AF434391

Stories of the American West
Volume 1

Rich Roy Thomson

Daniel Parliman

ISBN:979-8-218-12418-2 (Print version)
ASIN: B0BPMZBZB9 (Kindle version)

Published by Grizzly Creek Publishing
WWW.GrizzlyCreekPublishing.com

DEDICATION

Dedicated to my great Uncle, Robert Wilfred Thomson (1920-1973), and his father, Rich Roy Thomson (1881-1950), and his spouse Pearl Ellis Thomson (aka "Tommy") (1896-1970). I am also indebted to the experiences and hunting camp stories of my grandfather Henry DeCinque Sr (1909-2002) and my Uncle Henry DeCinque Jr (aka Nunny) (1938-2014) for their direct and indirect influences and stories while I was growing up.

I am very appreciative for my dear wife Connie, for all her love and support during the editing, writing, and production of this work.

CONTENTS

ACKNOWLEDGMENTS

Most importantly I want to acknowledge the late Rich Roy Thomson, for his short stories and his non-fiction article which are included in this work. I have no doubt that his spouse Pearl Ellis Thomson was very helpful in his writing as well, because by the time Rich died in 1950, he had lost his sight. His spouse, known to her family and friends as "Tommy" gave these almost completed stories to her son Robert, before her death in 1970. Probably because Robert, who had published some articles in Guns & Ammo Magazine in the late 1960s was a published author. Robert was quite involved in running his successful Glenwood Springs Restaurant "The Red Steer" at that time, as well as his lifelong side business of guiding elk and deer hunters into the Colorado Rockies. Unfortunately, Robert Thomson, passed away at the too-young age of 52 in 1973, his wife Jean Stanle Thomson faithfully kept all his papers together.

After Jean Thomson's death in 2016, these still unpublished works came to me, and after review, decided that they were worth the time and effort to edit and publish, and we hope you enjoy reading them.

In addition to the fictional western short stories, Rich had an article that described in detail, how the Thomson family organized their large and successful Wilderness trail rides of the 1930s-40s, which I felt should be included. This article, Rich titled as "The Last Roundup." The final work I included was an article I have written which attempts to summarize my experiences as a participant in the very last Thomson hunting camp, which took place over several months in the fall of 1972, when I was just age 16, turning 17, in the hunting area we called Ft. Defiance, located in the Colorado Flattops. Included in this are various hunting camp stories about the Thomson hunting camps through the years.

Suzzanne Bobo from western Colorado provided interesting background information on the John B. Schutte photograph collection, several key photos, and anecdotes about the trail rides, and I thank her for her efforts. Thanks to Dan Coffey and Zella Brink for their assistance via phone and/or text messages.

My brother, Dale Parliman, provided his information on some details that was very helpful.

During the review process, Barbara Parliman provided a review of many of the key parts of the book and made many suggestions for its improvement.

A big thank you to Rebecca Thomson, granddaughter of Rich and Tommy, for her family assistance in publishing some of these works, and for permission to use her Thomson family photographs of the trail rides.

Also like to thank the various friends and family members who took the time to review various portions of this work, and I treasure their help and comments.

Any remaining errors are mine alone.

THE SPOILING OF PLATEAU SAL
BY RICH ROY THOMSON

This story takes place during the early part of the new twentieth century. The Wright brothers of Dayton, Ohio, had not yet taken their historic flight. The West was still the West, even though Railroads now connected some of the major towns of Colorado's Western Slope. For at least 10 years, people could travel between the mining town of Aspen and the Grand Junction area by rail, even with one's horse in the livestock railcar. Some people still preferred to do that journey on horseback.

The "kid", sometimes called the "Aspen kid" was tired as he rode up the long slope, broke over the top of the ridge and looked down into the little Meadow Creek Valley—Meadow Creek is a branch of one of the many creeks cutting through the famous Plateau Valley in Western Colorado. This was near the Grand Mesa, north of Grand Junction. About One hundred and twenty years ago, this valley was one of the best cow countries of the West. A place where cattle were "King" and a country where many men were cowboys.

The time was spring with the aspen leaves just coming out; and the ground carpeted with a mat of brilliant, new spring grass. The robins had just started their spring-time evening serenade. Altogether, the kid thought the country beautiful—the spring flowers, a riot of color under foot, the music of the birds, the joy of life in the cool evening air. The kid was worried, though, and unhappy at the realization he was hungry, his saddle horse was leg weary, and he was in a strange country.

In three days, he had ridden from the mining camp of Aspen, far up in the mountains to the east and north. A cowboy he met in Glenwood Springs the night before had told him there should be several cow camps where one could hang up overnight on the creek valleys of the Buzzard, Plateau, or Meadow. His description of the country was vague. He didn't know whether someone had yet moved the cattle up from their winter home (in lower country) up to the higher grassy meadows. The kid's worry was a bit heightened by the fact he had seen no cattle since he had reached the high country. No cattle, no cowboys, no warm cabin with its supply of hot biscuits, ham, and fried spuds. In fact, it looked like he might not eat tonight; would have to "wolf it out". The thought of "wolfing" one night was not too bad; however, his planned route took him on far up the Meadow Creek to the crest of Colorado's Grand Mesa, thence down country to the nearest settlement of Cedaredge, on the south slope. It was a good day's ride from where he was then. He sat on his horse for a few moments, deliberating how his empty stomach would take another full day without food. The night would not be too bad, his horse on a picket rope and a good big fire to sleep by, more or less, but the kid's stomach bothered him. All winter he had worked in the mines at Aspen, eating three times a day. For ten days after leaving the mines, he had been out on a friend's ranch, helping break out a bunch of colts. With this strenuous activity and the accompanying three "squares" a day of ranch food, his stomach had not become accustomed to the dinnerless days of his summer life. He had just about decided he would turn down country and see if he could find a cow camp or ranch where he could "hang up", when a strange sound came rolling up from the valley below.

Strangely, mixed with the rumbling of wagon wheels rolling over a rocky road, was the singing voice of a man, a voice such as the kid had never heard before. In the evening's quiet air of the valley, the high notes of the song sang out like the sound of distant bells. The words were indistinguishable through the echo and repeated echoes ringing back from the mountain across the valley.

The kid touched the spurs to his horse and loped down the half mile slope toward the sound of the wagon and the song. Where that man stopped, there would be food, feed for his horse, and a warm bed. In those days, wherever man established himself, he provided a bed for those who might visit him, and food to supply the traveler's wants, whoever he might be. In the cow country, a man who failed in these little courtesies generally left within a year or so. His cows would come down in the fall with only the few calves he had branded before turnout time in the spring. His maverick colts would strangely disappear from their regular range, and if he found them and recognized them later, they carried a sleeper brand unknown to anyone in the county. Most men knew these grapevine consequences, or learned them quickly, so the kid was reasonably sure he was on the trail of bed and board.

Coming into the valley road fifty yards behind the wagon, he saw an enormous man sprawling over the seat. His entire head and half his back was covered by a Mexican type straw hat of a size never reached by the Mexican users. Hat on the back of the head, his face raised to the skies, he was singing a grand opera solo which the kid remembered hearing on his family's new talking machine.

"Why in the world doesn't that farmer try to make a living singing?", thought the kid as he rode to the wagon and out upon the hill alongside the team and stopped. The driver promptly pulled his team to a stop. "Howdy Mister", said the kid, "Do you know where my horse and me can hang up for the night?"

"Well, pardner, I shore do.", boomed the big man's musical voice. "I got a hoss camp a mile up the crick here, plenty of room. Git off your hoss and rest your saddle and ride with me."

The voice was kind, the smile of welcome very genuine, thought the kid as he slipped his lariat over his horse's neck and climbed to the seat beside the big fellow.

On the way to camp, the man introduced himself as Mate Styles, owner of the Indian Sign cow and horse outfit down the valley near Collbran, Colorado. The kid gave his last name, and his home as Aspen. Upon Mate's inquiry what line of work he followed, the kid said, "mining", and after some thought mentioned, he broke a few horses now and then. This delighted Mate, and in his enthusiasm for telling of his love for horses, he dropped his stagy western slang and broke into his life history. He was not a native of the region, in fact, had only been in

Colorado for a year. All during his life before he had been a singer, and several years ago had, in his early thirties, broke into the sacred ranks of the Metropolitan Opera. Having a little trouble with his lungs or throat a year before, his doctor told him to go west and stay for some time. This he had done, and at the advice of a friend, had come into the valley and bought the "Indian Sign" outfit. He had enjoyed so much fun, loved the country, its people and the life so well, he now planned to stay forever. In fact, he said, "I'm building a big horse pasture up at this camp, so I will have a place to keep my extra horses."

When they reached a new cabin that had been built high on the hill, and some distance from the running creek below, they were greeted by a cook and five or six cowboys. After an introduction to the boys at camp, the kid and Mate sat down to their late supper. The boys wandered off to one tent nearby for a poker game.

Partly through curiosity, and to make conversation, the kid asked why Mate had built the cabin so far up on the hill and away from the water.

"Well, I tell you it looks a little strange, but the echoes are wonderful up here, and I do like good singing. From the porch, I can sing out across the valley, stop, and listen to the echoes returning, and hear the voice of the finest singer in America."

The kid nodded understanding, although the unheard-of frank boasting of his host was a bit too sophisticated for his western training.

"Come out on the porch and I'll show you what I mean," said Mate, as the meal was finished.

Striking a pose on the edge of the cabin porch, the singer broke into a song, a song such as the kid had never heard before. The beautiful, powerful voice rang out in a single line, stopped abruptly. Then from the mountain on the opposite side of the valley came back, an echo so clear and distinct one thought it more beautiful than the first. Then, still a pause; and from far up the timbered mountain, miles away, faint, so sweetly clear, the kid thought of angel's voices. Surprised and unaccustomed tears blurred his eyes. Mate finished and dropped his enormous frame to a bench, tears rolling down each cheek.

"You see what I mean, kid?" his words a gentle sob, "The world may have lost the greatest voice it has ever known, but God willing, we'll always have it here with us." "You believe me, kid, I can see tears in your eyes."

The kid, unashamed, pulled his bandana out and wiped his eyes, then blew his nose loudly to hide his emotions. He glanced out at the tents. The poker crowd was outside, each with his cards in his hand. As they filed back into the tent, Mate nodded toward them.

"I know I can make the people of the outside world cry, but when I can bring tears to the eyes of such a hard twisted, cow stealing, bunch of cow punchers as that, I know I'm good."

The kid nodded his agreement.

Next morning at the breakfast table, Mate asked the kid if he wouldn't stay over a day and go fishing with him. "You need a little rest, besides your horse would enjoy the fine feed here in the pasture."

This last was an inducement no excellent horseman could resist, and the kid agreed. Then followed a series of questions by Mate, in fact, quite an oral examination.

Was he going over in the Delta County country to break horses? Had he broken many? How long had he been riding? Was he a pretty good or better-than-average rider? Was he a bronco buster?

The kid was embarrassed and modestly acknowledged he had ridden some number of broncs, and in his answer to the last question quietly replied: "Some people call me a bronco buster, so I guess I am."

This seemed to be what Mate was after, and as he glanced around the table at the listening cowboys, with more than a casual air, he said,

"I got an old mare out in the pasture. The boys sometimes ride, but she sometimes bucks a little. Would you mind riding her for me today before we go fishing?"

Every mouth in the room hung open for the kid's answer.

"I'll be glad to ride her for you, Mr. Styles," stated the kid.

Now this common pastime, or joke, of trying out new riders who professed to being a bronc rider, was probably new stuff to Mate, but old stuff to the kid. He had had it pulled on him as a much younger kid — had been bucked off several times from the "might buck a little" horses. Much water had gone under the bridge since those days, however, and much riding had been crowded into a few short years.

Most of the cowboys were sitting around the cabin waiting for the horse jingler to bring in the remuda of horses. The kid walked over toward the rear of the tent, and as he passed, he overheard one cowboy talking to the cook inside.

"It's a damn shame for Mate to put that kid up on Plateau Sal. No one has ever ridden her over three jumps. This kid isn't over nineteen or twenty and I would bet he doesn't weigh over 125 pounds. It's a damn shame."

The kid walked on, a faint smile on his lips.

The wranglers soon pushed the group of some forty horses in the corral. Mate's entire crew, normally pasture fence builders, perched around on the corral fence like rail birds at a rodeo. The kid went to his saddle and took down his rope and stepped into the corral of milling horses.

"What one do you want, Mr. Styles?" said the kid in a quiet and apparently half scared voice.

Mate was terribly excited and apparently somewhat conscience-stricken as he replied,

"Kid, maybe you had better not ride that mare. She might BUCK pretty hard." As he crawled down off the top corral pole, "That blazed, face? Big bay mare was the one," he pointed and said, "But I guess you had better ride that YT roan," turning and pointing to the opposite side of the corral.

The kid's loop shot out—not at the roan, but straight to the neck of the blazed face mare. A wild snort, one tremendous pawing leap at the rope stretching out toward the kid, and she came to a dead stop, turned, and in mincing steps approached the snubbing post and the rope. The kid, with a single motion from eight feet away, threw a couple of turns around the heavy snubbing post and hollered to the man at the gate,

"Let those others out."

Mate stood in openmouthed surprise and said not a word as the corral bars dropped and the remuda ran out. The big mare barely tightened the rope as the other horses left and stood quietly at the post. The kid stepped to his saddle and removed a hackamore and its long, soft braided bronc rein from his slicker roll. Stepping up to the quivering, wild-eyed, and snorting horse, he gently slid the hackamore over her nose and up over her ears and tied it down fast.

"How's this mare to saddle?" he inquired of one boy on the fence. "Will I have to but blinders on, or Scotch her?"

"She stands like a rock until you're on and try to start 'er," said the cowboy.

The kid picked up his saddle and touched the horse gently on the shoulder, sized up her tremendous brisket girth and set his saddle down. One of the boys came and held the hackamore rope while he let out his cinch to the last hole, then he gently slid it onto the mare's back. With a light of his lariat, he reached under and got the cinch, pulled it to him, and threaded the latigo, pulling it tight. The mare never made a move. Tightening his chap belt, he was apparently ready to mount, when Mate, white as a sheet, made one last appeal.

"Don't do it Kid, I'm afraid that mare is awful. I should have warned you. No one has ever ridden her—she's spoiled."

The kid, to whom this last statement was of such an obvious fact since he had cast his look over at her, replied dryly,

"Don't worry, Mr. Styles, if I can't ride her, I always light off easy. If I ride her, we'll go fishing."

With that, he pulled his big-four Stetson down tight on his forehead, stepped to the mare's head, with the coiled McCarty in his left hand, he grasped the neck rope and cheek pieces of the hackamore, pulled the mare's head slightly to the left, and stuck his extended forefinger in her eye.

The mare blinked and pulled her head away from the annoying finger. While thus distracting her attention, the kid's left foot kicked into the stirrup, high above his waist, the right hand at the same time grasped the saddle horn and the kid was mounted. No longer did he have that slightly worried and apologetic look. Maybe from the hard life, harder masters, and still a youth, the normal air of obedient humility was natural, perhaps assumed—it's hard to tell on some people.

But that's of no consequence; place any man on a good horse and if he understands the fundamentals of riding, he becomes immediately a knight in armor. Maybe the kid felt that way when he had a good bucking horse between his legs. He softly patted the neck of the quivering twelve hundred pounds of dynamite under him. His voice was still, but now with a command as sharp as a sting, "Let down those God D___ bars. Some of these punkin bellies may have learned to ride on skim milk calves in a tight corral, but damned if I did."

Mate made a futile protest. The cowboy at the gate dropped the bars.

The kid smiled at all the assembled cowboys. "Be seeing you," he said as he lifted the quirt from the saddle horn.

Stories differ about what happened next. Some boys say the kid slapped her on the shoulder with the quirt; others say he shot his heel halfway to her ears; dragged the spur rowel clear on back to the hip bone; some say both at once; some say the bawl she let out was heard three miles down the creek by some hands moving cattle. Anyway, it was a show talked of for many years in the Meadow Creek area. Like all tales that grow from year to year, it wasn't true that Plateau Sal bucked for a full two hours. She only bucked for about ten minutes close to the corral, but that was enough to give Mate a fainting spell as he watched the now deadly fight between the horse and man. The kid wasn't smiling when Mate passed out. White as a sheet, grim lips closed in desperation, the kid and horse were fighting to a finish. Plateau Sal, in her ten salty years, had met nothing like this. Neither had the kid. In his brief life, he had either been bucked off, or long before this had felt the falter and give-up signs of the ordinary bronc. He was wondering, "Can I really stick it out?"

Plateau Sal, with her tongue outside her wide-open mouth, continued to bawl in hate and terror. The kid's spurred heels never stopped their rhythmic swing, shoulder to flank, one side with the mare's jump, the other side with the next jump. On her sweat and lather covered sides, each mark of the spurs showed clearly, crisscrossed with the mark of the stinging quirt as it lashed from one shoulder to the other with each lunging plunge.

When Mate collapsed and fell off the corral fence, the screaming yell of the cook, sitting next to him, brought every man off the fence and in a race toward his body. This spooked the bucking mare or gave her an excuse to quit bucking and break into a wild stampede off toward the heavy willows along the creek. Only after one of the boys filled his hat with water from the nearby stream, dashed it over Mate's face, the face gasping out as he recovered consciousness, "Is he still on?", did the boys think of this question? One ran to a nearby saddled horse, mounted, and tore out in the direction the mare had taken.

In twenty minutes, the cowboy returned. Following meekly, twenty feet behind was Plateau Sal, still sweating and her front quarters covered with crimson foam, both nostrils dripping a few drops of blood. Atop her sat the kid, flushed faced and smiling, full of confidence and with no injuries other than a few bloody scratches across his face. They rode into the corral and the kid stepped down off the mare, patted her face a few times, and walked over to the group of cowboys at the gate.

A grizzled old bow-legged cowpuncher gravely reached out his hand and said, "Young feller, I want to shake hands with you. That's the damnest bucking horse I ever saw, and you sure rode her Cheyenne rules."

The others walked up silently and shook hands, the kid's eyes only showing the triumph and pleasure he felt at the compliments of these men who knew what they spoke of. Mate's joy was greater and more demonstrative. Grabbing the kid's hand with both of his, he shook until the kid's teeth chattered.

"Come work for my outfit. I'll pay you more than anyone in this country. What a show we can put on with you and Sal."

The kid smiled a bit strangely, and replied, "Perhaps, sometime. I promised to work out a bunch of colts over on the Uncompahgre, and of course, I got to go there first."

Mate and the kid spent most of the day fishing, the little stream being alive with hungry little red cutthroat trout.

Mate told the kid of his plans. He was building the Meadow Creek pasture as a place to hold what he hoped would be the worst bunch of spoiled horses in the west, or to put it the other way, the best bunch of hard bucking outlaws that money could buy.

"You know with you to ride Plateau Sal as the feature event, and other bronco snappers to ride the others, I believe we can take 'em back and clean up with a rodeo show in that there Madison Square Garden."

The kid agreed it was a good idea, but with an unspoken thought that the dudes from the east sure had some screwball and fantastic ideas.

As the kid prepared to leave camp the next morning, Mate drew him aside. "I've been giving the boys down in the Valley $25.00 each for trying to ride that mare. You rode her to a standstill, and I want to give you $50.00."

The kid shook his head. "No thanks, Mr. Styles. Out here, we like to do little favors like topping-off a bronc for our friends, and we don't think of charging for it." A little embarrassed pause, "If you could spare me a pack of those store made cigarettes, I would sure appreciate that." Mate quickly produced, and the Kid pocketed a couple of packs.

He waved a thankful "goodbye" and rode on up the Meadow Creek trail.

More than six months later...

Late that fall, and the evening before the annual race meet and rodeo was to start, a young lady and her escort came into the big Katie Bender restaurant in Glenwood Springs. The girl was a gushing young blonde with a low hung peach basket hat, a mode of the day. The young man was a slim young fellow with a stiff derby hat, pleated stiff white shirt, a high wing collar, loud silk socks and patent leather shoes, also the modes of the day; except his dark tanned skin, looked like any of the hundred other small-town dandies, walking about the town in their Sunday best.

The couple took a table in the corner and were busy trying to decide what they wanted to eat when six booted and spurred cowboys came in and took a table nearby. All had consumed a few drinks and were talking louder than necessary. Recognizing a voice, he had heard before, the kid turned and glanced over at the group. Seated at the head of the table was one cowboy he had met at the Mate Styles camp the previous spring.

Yes, it was the same kid I was telling you about. With saddle, chaps,

Stetson, Levi's, and boots packed in the luggage trunk in his room, he felt sure the cowboy would not recognize him in the "dude" clothes— and he hoped he wouldn't.

Cocking an ear toward the cowboy, as the name of Mate Style's was mentioned, he listened closely. The cowboy went on with his story amid a storm of uproarious laughter from his companions.

"Mate had old Plateau Sal up at the horse camp where we was a-building fence last Spring. Along came this young feller one evening they call the "Aspen Kid", looking like a half-grown schoolboy, hardly dry behind the ears. Mate boned him to ride Plateau Sal, and the kid accepts. He rode her, Cheyenne rules, not only rode her, but scratched and quirted the living tar out of her. A few months later, along about the fourth of July, Buffalo Bill's show was showing in Denver and Bill heard about this horse, Sal. He wired Mate he would give a thousand bucks for her if she was the bucker they claimed.

Along came his horse buyer and top bronco stomper. Mate meets 'em at the ranch. They saddled Sal, and the guy got on. Sal acted just like she always done, quiet as a lamb until the stomper kicked her on the shoulder. Instead of exploding, Sal just broke into a lumbering lope, looked hurt at the scratching and quirting she was getting. Not a jump could her rider get. Bill's men left in disgust and Mate nearly had a hemorrhage. He got several of the other boys to try her out and never a jump could they get, even though Mate put up $25 a piece for a couple of lopes around the corral. He finally hitched her up and put her to pulling a haying wagon; she's the gentlest work horse he's got. That kid sure spoiled an awful, good bucking horse."

Several Decades later...

"How come you know all about this, Dad?" the narrator's young son asked.

"Well," said the old timer with a faraway smile, "I married that Kid's wife."

THE END.

Rich wrote the above short story in the years before his death in 1950. During the early 1900s, he was a very successful rodeo cowboy in Colorado, and held other ranch jobs, as well as some mining jobs. In 1907 he joined the US Forest Service. Prior to this, he was very successful in many rodeos throughout Colorado, and is believed to have won at least one rodeo where he was designated: "Saddle Bronc Champion of the World".

His wife, the former Pearl Ellis, a blonde, was a renowned horse woman in her own right, and was very involved in the couple's successful horse business and a driving force of the Thomson family business of Hunting Camps and summer Wilderness Trail rides in the period from the late 1920s into the early 1950s.

Their sons, James and Robert, were involved in the family business when not following their careers. James was very involved in the trail rides during the early days and later became Chief Engineer of Stearns and Rogers Mining and Manufacturing company. Robert, when not involved in his Navy job, or later running his restaurants; concentrated on running Hunting Camps from the late 1940s until the very last one, in 1972.

More about Pearl, Robert, and James in Rich's article "The Last Roundup", and about Robert in "The Last Thomson Hunting Camp"

THE LOST BOY GOLD LODE
BY RICH ROY THOMSON

There are many stories of valuable gold or silver mines, usually found by some old prospector in the far dim past. Unfortunately, its location was lost to the world through the untimely death of the old fellow, but this chase for gold or treasure still excites the interest of adventurous people throughout the west. Here is my saga.

Back in the 1880s and early 1890s, in the mining camp of Aspen, Colorado, mining and related interests were the focus around which much of the community interests centered. Rich strikes were made by poor men, and they within a few days became rich men. Rich men invested their fortunes in likely looking mining properties, then became poor men when they failed to find paying ore. Small wonder everyone was allergic to the hope of ever finding a mine when one of Aspen's silver mines produced the largest single piece of silver ever found in the history of mining, in 1894, of over 1800 pounds of silver in one nugget! They had also found rich strikes at nearby Lenado, far over the hills to the north near Woody Creek, and richer ores at Ashcroft, far to the south. Prospecting for more and greater finds was in the thoughts of thousands; several hundred prospectors diligently carried out actual prospecting activities throughout the summer months. Unless a paying mine property was found during the summer, development work started, little was said or claimed of their findings by the prospector. Let the heavy fall snows pile up to two or three feet in depth, forcing the men into town and the cheering warmth of hot spiced toddies, sipped in their favorite easy chairs at the Buckhorn, or the Red Onion, then one could hear fabulous tales of their summer discoveries.

Some men were quiet and secretive, with their every action giving the impression that they had "found it" and were lying low until spring. Others in a more desperate situation, "in their cups", as the expression goes, earnestly told their listeners, "The greatest find since the Mollie Gibson," (Aspen's richest mine) or "a second Cripple Creek". Each one alike, the quiet, or the loudest braggart, carried an ore glass and an ore specimen in his pocket, willing to show at any time or place. Many, or at least a few of these rich ore specimens, had originally come from the Little Annie, the Spar, the Mollie Gibson of Aspen. Possibly from the more distant mines of Leadville, Cripple Creek, or the San Juan, which made little difference. They were rich in silver or gold, and no "doubting Thomas" could prove they came not from the prospector's claim.

Some prospectors were honest, hardworking and of excellent character, as evidenced by their securing a job in the local mines and saving their money for a summer's grub stake.

Others were opportunists, although that word was little known and seldom used in those days, and those boys got by the best they could during the long winter months.

The experiences of Horace Tabor at Leadville (he of Silver King fame), and his outlay of small, inexpensive grub stakes which brought him millions, were fresh in the memory of many in the mining camps of the 1890s. Some prospectors with a cabin in which to live secured their winter supplies from a friendly grocer, with a promise of a share in the next summer's findings; others secured meal tickets and room rent from prosperous saloon keepers or a mine lessor who was in a good ore position, and thus able to stake someone.

Occasionally one of the old boys of the hills gave up the uncertainties of prospecting and life and crossed the "Great Divide". In nine cases out of ten, this unfortunate event gave birth to a new and mysterious lost mine story, and true to form, or the formula, in time grew into a "true lost mine story"—Like the Lost Dutchman's Mine, down in Arizona.

Small wonder that a young man brought up in such a country, in a community where the mining of the rich deposits of ore was the primary industry; the discovery of new deposits, an ambition of all, should be a natural prospector.

My friend Hod and I were like all the other young fellows in their teens.

We were wise in mining methods and familiar with the appearance of many kinds of ore. We probably did more prospecting than the other young fellows and tried to investigate more of the lost mine locations than any of the others. We always kept a few saddles and pack horses on hand, to do a little prospecting when a likely opportunity would arise.

One summer, a logging company employed us in the construction of a logging chute to be used in bringing timber off the slopes of Smuggler Mountain near Aspen to the sawmill site on the Roaring Fork River.

Our employer was being "staked" by a small business merchant in town, and nearly always was short of funds, and even short of a sufficient food supply for his logging crew. For days, the camp had been entirely out of fresh meat, and the entire crew of about ten men had grown tired of their salt or smoked meat diet. Hod and I were not only tired of the grub, but we were also tired of the steady grind of ten hours of work each day and longed for a few days of freedom.

In the presence of the boss one morning, Hod mentioned he would surely like to have one of the nice fat mountain sheep that were so plentiful up in the area near Maroon Lake. The boss said nothing then, but shortly afterward, called Hod and me into his office. He inquired as to the abundance of the sheep, how large they were, and how tasty they might be to eat. Our glowing account as to the fine sweet meat of the mountain rams, the ease with which we could find and kill a pair of the animals, and at night pack the skinned-out carcasses back to camp, finally prompted the offer we had been waiting for.

"If you two can bring back two sheep and place them in the meat house, I'll give you three days off with regular pay."

Hod and I were happy—we had only the evening before considered playing hooky from our job for a few days, of course, taking the chance of getting fired and certainly losing our pay for the absent days. Our crew chief made the offer just before wash time in the morning, and I lost no time in asking if we could start that day. The boss readily agreed to this, adding that he too was getting pretty well fed up on a straight diet of salty pork.

Our horses were at a ranch scarcely a half mile from the camp. Catching them up, saddling our two saddle horses and a couple of pack horses, and returning to the camp took little more than an hour's time.

The cook gave us several days of grub, and with our guns, fish poles, and beds, we soon packed up and were underway. Six miles down the river to Aspen, thence the eight or nine miles to the forks of Maroon Creek, were covered by around two in the afternoon. The camp setup was on the east side of the creek just below the forks of the two creeks, one from Maroon Lake, the other heading far to the south.

We spent the afternoon fishing and planned on making our hunt the following day. In those days, Maroon Creek at that distance from town was alive with toothsome, little, red-throated, native cutthroat trout, and in a few hours, we had several days' supply. This was despite that Hod and I ate six to eight apiece at a meal. We were growing boys.

Early the next morning, we cleaned our rifles, each a 38-55 caliber with the new smokeless powder loads and mushroom bullets. The guns were single-shot weapons, the kind that had to be reloaded with each shot. We would carry our extra cartridges in our pants pockets for easy reloading.

Just after the old East Maroon stage road leaves the creek bottom, and just below the forks of the creek, there is a long open snow slide gulch (small valley) leading up the mountain on the east. Several times in the past, Hod and I had found pieces of a reddish-colored quartz float rock in this gulch, and as it offered an easy climb to the higher country where bighorn sheep often were found in those days, we chose it as our route. As we climbed higher, we found more and more of the red quartz, and some small pieces of grey quartz. The entire country nearby appeared to be of lime and sandstone formation and quartz, very rare.

At about timberline, or slightly above, as I remember, we found much of the quartz float, and off to the left side of the gulch, as we ascended, we found a well-defined vein of the material. Emptying our pockets of the float material, we broke off several specimens of both the red and grey quartz and filled our pockets. Noting the location well, we again went about our business of getting meat for the camp.

This was not difficult; within a quarter of a mile from the quartz lode or vein, we spotted three nice young rams and soon made a stalk and killed two of them. With short pieces of rope tied to the horns, after hog dressing, we dragged the carcasses down the mountain to the old stage road. Picking them up with a pack horse and taking them into camp was a minor job and by noon we had them skinned out and hung in the shade for cooling. During the afternoon, Hod and I took turns in fanning the flies away and letting the meat hang until dark when it had thoroughly cooled.

We placed the meat in large flour sacks, brought along for the purpose. Then we put the sacks in our panniers, careful to keep the weight balanced, and we were ready to start the long ride back to the logging camp. This we did at night, partly to keep the meat in good condition, but possibly a better reason might have had something to do with our decision. We were not totally sure if Mountain Sheep were in season, so thought it best to come back to camp at night, just to be sure.

Just before dark, my friend and I emptied our pockets and prepared to place our ore specimens in the panniers. At first glance at one of the grey quartz specimens, I fairly yelled in excitement, "For God's sake, look at this, Hod."

In my hand, I held a specimen half the size of an egg. Splattered over a freshly broken side of the rock was a dazzling picture of bright yellow free gold. Gold ore such as I had seen from the rich Cripple Creek mines, high-grade specimens stolen and smuggled out by the miners. We examined more of the specimen and found free gold on nearly every rock. I took a camp ax and broke one piece of rock. Strange, strange to say, not a speck could we detect in the freshly broken faces of the rock. I rushed over to my chaps and in the pocket found my magnifying ore glass. In the fast-fading light, I examined the gold with the powerful glass. I stared and stared, Hod impatiently waiting his turn to look through the glass. When I finally handed the glass to Hod, he must have seen the look of cruel disappointment on my face. He gave one close look, and as I saw the shock of his discovery, come over his face, I laughed. He laughed, and we joined in uproarious laughter, strangely close to tears. We were still kids, maybe older and tougher than our years, but we were still kids. Even old men sometimes shed tears openly, when they see a fortune fade away before their very eyes.

The powerful ore glass showed clearly where the bright brass of our polished cartridge shells had rubbed off on the rougher quartz faces.

We looked through the bunch of specimens and threw away those which showed the brass scratches clearly, except for a half dozen brass-marked samples we kept to the side, just in case we wanted to have fun with our friends. We then dumped the balance in one duffle bag.

The long ride through the night to Aspen, up its alleys and back streets, and on to camp, was accomplished without incident. We unpacked and placed the meat in the camp "meat house", returned our horses to the ranch pasture, and were back in our bunks before daylight.

The next morning, we "slept in" and did not arise until noon. In fact, it was the wonderful odor of the juicy brown roast the cook removed from the cook's Dutch oven that did the trick.

The crew expressed little interest in our trip. They all knew or suspected that we had brought in the meat, and as there were scarcely any deer in the Aspen region in those days, they undoubtedly knew what it was. Men did not ask too many embarrassing questions. They ate, and we all enjoyed the meat without comment. Each man's business was his own, and his alone.

Hod and I rested the balance of the day. After supper, all the men were seated out on the benches in front of the bunkhouse. Hod mentioned to one man we had found good-looking quartz, and he asked to see it. Bringing out a piece of the rock from the duffle bag, Hod handed it to the man. We both watched him closely, expecting to have a lot of fun with our brass-marked ore joke. The man casually examined the piece of rock, suddenly turned pale, and glanced around at the other men nearby. None were paying any attention to him, all listening intently to an exciting story the boss was telling. The man arose and started rapidly toward the camp outhouse, to the rear of the bunkhouse. When he had passed beyond the view of the other men, he turned and excitedly beckoned Hod and me. We followed him behind the buildings, and he turned in wild excitement, so much so that he could hardly speak.

"My God, boys, did you know that rock is fairly filled with gold?"

Then followed an incoherent volley of questions. "Where did we find it? Does anyone else know about it? Did we know we were rich?" He said, "Could he get in, somehow?"

This was more than Hod and I had bargained for. The man acted like a maniac. He was a tough old ex-miner, a man of violent temper. Hod and I did not feel that this was the time or place to disclose our little joke. We were scared stiff at the developments. We told him our lode was far up in the mountains, with a wave to the south; no one else knew about it; we did not know how rich the ore was; yes, we might let him in on it somehow. He pledged us to secrecy—and assumed the air of now being our partner. Before we returned to the bunkhouse, he made the last offer to clinch the bargain. "I've got $200 saved over the past year to grub stake me on a prospecting trip to Arizona this winter. I'll lay off tomorrow and go to town and get it for you. It's all yours if you will just promise to let me take up a claim alongside yours. Do not tell a soul."

He returned our specimens with a warning to take them to town in the morning and place them in the bank.

"That stuff is better than any high grade in Cripple Creek—it's valuable."

Hod and I walked down the road that evening and talked over our find. Maybe that old miner did see some gold in it. Maybe we had better take it to town and cache it in a safe place and have it assayed.

We asked the boss to let us lay off the next day, and our request was granted. "Old Frank", our new mining partner, wanted to go down with us to get his $200, but we discouraged the plan and said to him he could pay later. We picked up our total supply of "gold" and rode our horses down to Aspen.

Traveling to my home, we got out an old mortar and pestle, a small steel pot-like container, and a heavy steel pestle, or crusher, and built something like an old-fashioned potato masher with a rounded face and ground up about a third of our ore supply into a fine dust. This we placed in a tobacco sack and took to one of the local ore assayers for analysis. By late afternoon, we had received the return from the assayer; the assay showed a trace of gold. Once before, Hod and I had ground up an old empty brown whiskey jug and had it assayed. This also showed a trace of gold, and when we confronted the assayer with our joke, he calmly stated, "nearly every rock he had ever seen would show this trace of gold when assayed". He added that nearly all mineral water and all seawater would show similar results.

Hod and I were not shocked at the showing of the sample, however, we were concerned about what our self-styled mining partner would think. We knew that ore showing the amount of free gold our "salted specimens" had apparently shown to the naked eye would run to many thousand dollars per ton of value. We hesitated to take back to camp the assay return as we knew our miner friend would know there was something wrong somewhere. A bright idea came to mind. In my small mineral collection, I had a piece of grey high-grade quartz a friend had brought over from Cripple Creek and given to me. Why not give "Old Frank" this specimen for "his own", and let him enjoy his and our secret, and we would never have to tell of our playful hoax? This seemed a very good and charitable solution to the problem. The Cripple Creek ore sample looked nearly exactly like the grey, Maroon Creek quartz we had shown to him, and we could see no flaw or harm in making the exchange. This specimen we gave him, upon our return to camp, hiding in my barn all the specimens of the brass-marked quartz exhibit except one small piece. I showed this to my dad at supper that evening. He was tremendously excited about the find until we told him of the brass and our neutral assay return.

Dad was a great joker, and immediately said, "Let me take this down to the office this evening and I will have some fun with the boys."

Like Hod and I, Dad did not at the time realize to what an extent a joke about gold might reach and took the specimen with him to the office after supper. Sure enough, my dad, Alden S. Thomson, who was an editorial writer for the Aspen Daily Times, then published by B. Clark Wheeler, showed the rich gold ore to the entire office group and told of two unknown boys who had found it. There was considerable excitement around the print shop that evening, and Dad was enjoying the joke immensely. He had intended to tell the boys the entire story later in the evening but became engrossed in the deep subject of his night's editorial writing and forgot the matter. Shortly after midnight, he returned home and went to bed.

Sometime around seven a.m., the paper was delivered to our door, and Mother went out to get it. Clear across the top of the front page and in the largest newspaper type the paper had on hand, was the headline caption, "ASPEN, A GOLD CAMP." Following and occupying several columns was one of the most thrilling and mysterious stories of a fabulous gold discovery that the state of Colorado had ever known.

Riland, a miner, prospector, reporter, and later publisher of the White River Review, was a reporter of the old school. First, he performed a brief examination of the "gold studded rock specimen" and then listened to Dad's mysterious and short explanation of its discovery. This enabled Jimmy Riland to write a wondrous tale. As he explained at the end of his long article, much secrecy was necessary by the lucky prospectors in order that they could make surveys and perfect the title of their claims.

Mother, who had seen our quartz and had heard us tell Dad of the brass-marked rock, rushed in, and awakened him, paper in hand.

It horrified my father at his failure to enlighten the office men, and hurriedly dressing, went to the office, immediately. B. Clark was in the office where he shared a desk with Dad and was just finishing reading Jimmy's story. "Just what we need—just what the district needs." he exclaimed, and continued, "Aspen has a world of silver, but we need gold to make it the greatest camp in the world."

 Dad finally got in a word, and in complete and broody silence, B. Clark listened to the story and Dad's apology that he had forgotten to tell the office boys, the complete true story. As he finished, Dad stated, "In tomorrow's paper, I'll tell the complete story and take the blame."

"Like H---l you will," said B. Clark, "That news story will appear in every paper in the state of Colorado tomorrow, and the following week will see it all over America. We need it, the country needs it. True or false, it will stir up the mining excitement we need, and it is sensational news, man!" "You are an old newspaperman, and you know it's the best news item we have had in our paper for years." He paused for breath. "Let's see the specimen."

Dad fished it out of his vest pocket and handed it to the boss. B. Clark turned to his desk drawer and pulled out a powerful ore glass. He gave one long look, turned, and threw the rock into the burning coals of an open stove door.

"Ten thousand miners and mining men with capital will invade this camp within a month. We need more miners, and we need more mining investors. You're a mighty fine editorial writer and I'd hate to lose you. You're too damn honest and truthful for a mining man or a promoter. If anyone asks you a word about this story or the ore, refer them directly to me." As an afterthought, "Don't let your kid spill the beans, either."

Dad agreed. There was only one daily paper in Aspen, and Dad liked his job and loved living in Aspen.

He hurried home and hitched up the family buggy horse and drove to our Roaring Fork camp. Getting permission from our boss to call us from our work, he recounted the results of his own little joke. He was in deadly earnest as he said to Hod and I the hoax must go no further, but in no case must it be disclosed to a soul. We gave our promise to my dad and returned to work.

That afternoon, the backer and promoter of our logging project came up to camp with a grub supply, and in his spring wagon had a copy of the morning paper. The boss grabbed it up and read the entire story to the men at the dinner table. "Old Frank", open-mouthed and looking like a thundercloud, looked across the table at Hod and me, laid his forefinger on his lips, and shook his head, time after time as he caught our eyes. All were excited but strange to say. No one seemed to connect Hod and me, or our mysterious meat trip, with the gold discovery.

Frank got us to one side at the first opportunity. He said, "My God, boys, what have you done, and what have you said to others?"

I explained we had given my dad a piece of the quartz, and he had shown it to the newspapermen. Dad had not known where we had found the gold, and had not, and would not tell a soul that we were the discoverers. This seemed to appease him somewhat, but it surprised us to see him a short time later get in the spring wagon and drive off with the backer on his return trip to town. We had given him the gold specimen from Cripple Creek the night before, and we wondered if he might go down to get an assay from it.

We never saw "Old Frank" again. His bed and belongings remained around camp all summer, and his two weeks' wages due were never claimed. Only after many years did we hear the true story of his disappearance and learned that other Aspen prospectors who also rushed up to Alaska when the gold strike hit the news, had seen "Old Frank" up in the Alaska gold fields. From the developments of a few days later, and the story I learned many years afterward, I'll try to piece out the missing facts.

"Old Frank" went directly to the assay office and had the assayer "try out" a piece of the specimen we had given him. The man pledged to absolute secrecy before the test was made, and by late evening had completed an assay that showed the rock to carry hundreds of ounces of gold to the ton with values of many thousands of dollars. With the assay card in his possession, duly dated, certified, and signed by the most reliable chemist in the town, "Old Frank" went to the leading big-time gambler of Aspen. The town was buzzing with the excitement of the new gold strike. The miners gathered at the bars and discussed the possibility of this or that locality being the scene of the find, or this or that prospector being the lucky man.

In the meantime, "Old Frank" went to the office of the gambler and showed his assay return. He pledged him to complete secrecy, showed him the half section of the Cripple Creek rock he had kept, and made his proposal. "Old Frank" confirmed he had found an enormous body of the ore mentioned in the paper, and for ten thousand dollars, he would make the gambler an equal partner in all his claims, then held or thereafter filed upon. He needed the cash immediately to hire a bodyguard, in the event the secret of his identity as the discoverer might creep out, and to prevent being kidnapped; to hire surveyors to run the claim lines, and to hire good lawyers to make his claims safely and legally contest proof.

The gambler thought it over. He thought of the tremendous fortunes being made by lucky mine owners; and thought how much better to be a wealthy mine owner than his current life of uncertainty as a gambler. He was a gambler now, however, and decided quickly. "Wait here a few minutes," he said and left the office, going to an office a block away, a lawyer of high renown in mining litigation. The gambler instructed the lawyer to draw up a partnership agreement that would hold in any court of law. After about a half hour, the lawyer prepared the document in the latest legal form, using his own typewriter, and after both had read the agreement, then he and "Old Frank" left to find the judge.

Luckily, the Judge was easy to find in his normal late afternoon poker game. He witnessed the signature as a notary public and signed the agreement following the signature of "Old Frank" and the gambler. He left and returned to his poker game.

The gambler placed his copy of the partnership in the safe and removed $10,000 from its place in the strongbox. This was the "bankroll", also called "the sack", the supply of funds to back up the various games of the establishment. All in comparatively small bills, it made up a huge roll. The gambler suggested Frank leave it there with him until the bank opened in the morning, but Frank promptly and vetoed this proposal. "I've done my part fair and square. You're supposed to be a straight shooter, and I want my money now."

The gambler knew these old miners and their peculiar way of thinking, and he handed the money over in several bulky packages. Frank unrolled the money and laboriously counted it to the last dollar. Placing it in his shirt front, he arose and with a cool, "See you tomorrow", left the room.

The gambler rushed into a card room and called to the armed official bouncer of the place. He told him to follow "Old Frank" and see that he gets to his room at the hotel. "Stay in the lobby all night and see that he doesn't leave."

He provided no more explanation, and none asked. The man carried out his instructions and saw Frank get his key and go to his room. He sat in the lobby throughout the night, reading and thinking of what an easy shift his assignment had turned out to be.

At ten o'clock the next morning, the gambler arose, and after breakfast, walked over to the hotel. The guard was still there, waiting for relief or further instructions. "Old Frank" had not arisen, nor had he appeared in the lobby, and the men left. After lunch, the gambler again went to the hotel. The clerk said Frank had not been down, but he would call him if his visitor wished to see him. After a brief discussion at the front desk, they sent the hotel bellboy up, but soon returned with the statement that the door appeared locked, and even a heavy pounding got no answer. The gambler was a little worried. "Old Frank" held ten thousand dollars of what had been his money, and he held only a receipt and contract agreement. He asked the clerk if he would go up with him and try to arouse the sleeping man. They found the door locked, and repeated calls and knocking brought no response. The clerk bent down to see if he could see through the keyhole, quickly arose, and inserted a passkey in the hole. The door quickly opened, and they gazed across to the vacant bed. "Old Frank" had not slept in that bed, and the pillows with their stiff starched surfaces were as smooth as was the unmade bed. The clerk stared a moment. "Must have gone out last night down the back stairs. Probably drunk somewhere."

The gambler said three little words, softly, sadly, but with the never say die expression of a true gambler, "A lousy misdeal."

Not for many years, until the tempering and soothing effects of time gave humor to the story or his outlook on it, did he mention his bargain with "Old Frank".

That same day, however, he started a silent but persistent search for his partner. The gambler sent a rider to the logging camp, but no one there had seen him since he left the day before. During the next two weeks, he hired men to ride all the out-of-the-way trails leading to the hills. No one understood his interest in finding "Old Frank". Some thought it a humanitarian interest of a wealthy man for his old prospector friend. About two weeks after "Old Frank's" disappearance from his hotel room, the hotel received a hotel room key in an envelope postmarked from San Francisco. Frank was always honest that way.

The gambler stopped all searching activities when the hotel clerk told him about Frank's room key being received. "A lousy misdeal" was his only comment.

In the meantime, miners and investors continued to pour into the camp. B. Clark was happy. Several invested heavily in his Little Annie and Midnight claims, and new and richer silver strikes were made in a few of his other claims.

The town assayer got on a spree and while down in his cups and announced the fabulous values in a sample "Old Frank" had given him before his disappearance.

At the logging camp, all was going along much in its usual manner until the assayer's story of the rich gold assay appeared in the newspaper.

That night, the boss called Hod and me into his office. He was all business and went directly to the point. "You boys read the paper today and saw about "Old Frank's" gold assay. He hasn't been away from here all summer. I remember the day you boys got back from hunting, you showed him some ore, and he pulled out for town the next day. What do you know about it?"

Hod and I were dumbfounded; he seemed to know more than he should. He acted as if he might be at the point of accusing us of killing the old man. I immediately said to him we had given "Old Frank" a piece of ore we had found but did not disclose the fact that we had substituted Cripple Creek ore for that found in Maroon Gulch. The questioning then turned to where we had found the specimen given to Frank.

"We tramped both forks of Maroon Creek far and wide looking for those sheep we brought back to camp. Somewhere in the two days I found the quartz but don't have the least idea where I picked it up." I delivered this speech with all the straightforwardness I could muster. If he believed it, I never knew.

"Someday I'll go up with you boys and we'll try to find the place," and he dismissed us.

Not long afterward, Hod and I have a nice camp grubstake earned, somewhat irked by the confinement of a steady job and hard work, drew our time and pulled out. Yes, you guessed it right the first time. We loaded our grub and outfit and pulled out for Maroon Creek. With its thousands of young fat grouse, fish trying to jump into your frying pan, wild raspberries, strawberries, and mushrooms for the picking, and fresh sweet meat of mountain sheep in a few minutes; where could one go to a better place?

The story seeped out from the logging camp, or from other leaks, that the two kids with "Old Frank" had found the rich gold ore and were up in Maroon trying to find the place again. We profited mightily from the many prospectors and miners who came up and camped for a few days while searching for "The Lost Boy Gold Lode". These fellows always brought twice enough grub and always left at our camp what they could not use.

The years went by. Hod and I grew into men and went our different ways, but the story of the "Lost Boy Gold Lode" did not die. As through the years, the details became dim, and local people forgot, other details were supplied and enlarged. From far distant places, the revised story became better known than nearby.

During the Great War, what the folks now call World War I, I was working at a small dry placer mining project in an isolated section of the Arizona desert. Going into the bunkhouse one evening, I sat down and listened to a crew of desert rat prospectors discussing lost mine legends. I sat back in the shadows and listened intently. After the Lost Dutchman, Plata La Platos, and other well-known lost mine sagas were told, an old prospector made me lean forward and strain to hear every word.

"I've got the awful straight dope on the old "Lost Boy Gold", way up in the mountains of Colorado. A long time ago, a couple of kids were out hunting from Aspen, rich silver diggings. These kids broke a piece of ore off a ledge and took it to town. They say it was half gold. The kids went back and hunted all summer but couldn't find it again. They came back summer after summer for many years but could never find it." He stopped and took a fresh chew of tobacco. "Well, sir, I met a Navajo sheepherder who had herded sheep up in those parts where the boys were lost. He told me he had found the ledge, but being an Injun, could not file a claim in those days. We were all set to go up together last year when the Injun up and died on us. We made up a little map afore he died, and I believe I kin find the ore."

I said nothing before the crowd. These old fellows take their stories and themselves seriously and one must use tact in getting along with them. Later, when he and I were out on a job together, I said to him the complete story of the "Lost Boy Gold Lode" and noted his disappointment, along with a slight air of disbelief.

I asked if I might see the map he spoke of and he promptly refused. I immediately apologized for making such a request and assured him my only interest was that of curiosity, and that, having lived at Aspen for many years, I might help him improve his map. He thought a moment and said, "Young Feller, I believe you're honest and would not try to rob an old man, so I'll show you."

After supper that evening, he came over to my place and drew a folded sheet of paper from his coat pocket. On a ruled sheet of cheap pencil-drawn paper was a map. A wondrous map of a type I had never seen. With all its queer make-up, there, as accurately as I could have located it on a conventional map, was an **"X"** marking the location of our barren quartz ledge. I explained to the old gentleman that the map was correct, that anyone could find this ledge, but I was sorry that the quartz was barren, and had only shown the brass cartridge marks.

"Well thanks, young feller, I always wanted to see Colorado and I guess I'll go up next spring. They say there's water in every gulch." — and that was that; someone cannot discourage easily a lost mine hunter.

Ten or twelve years later, one morning I was saddling up and preparing to pack out from my horse corral near the outskirts of Glenwood Springs. This was a regular procedure, as I left my home to attend to my duties as the district forest ranger. Looking down across the road to my neighbor's corral, I saw him also packing up a horse. This was an unusual procedure for him. However, a doctor with a busy practice rarely did he have the opportunity for a camping trip.

Crossing the road and entering his corral, I asked, "Where do you think you are going, Doc?"

He looked at me a moment and then replied, "It's a secret and I wish you wouldn't repeat it, I can hardly spare the time, but—" and he walked up close, "I've got some dead sure dope on that old "Lost Boy Gold Lode" above Aspen. Old Man R____, before he died, gave me the exact location, and I can't afford to not go up and find it."

Now Doc was an excellent friend of mine, and he took it well when I told him the "whole story", and fairly rolled on the ground in laughter. He never liked me so well since and does not care to discuss the case.

I expected him to unsaddle, but he went right along with his packing, as I stood around, a little hurt at his coolness and disregard for my story. He eased the situation somewhat, and said, "You know, I've always wanted to go up into that Maroon Creek Country, and so long as I am ready, I'm going." — So that was that again. You just can't knock down these lost mine stories, nor can you dampen the spirits of those who wish to hunt for treasure.

Several Generations Later

Now there is the "Plates of Silver" mine in Arizona. I don't believe in most of the old lost mine legends, never did very much, but the mines of the silver plates were real. In 1934, I found what I consider is the actual truth about its location, and if I can get someone to go down there with me sometime, I'm sure we'll find it.

"But Dad, where is the old ledge in Maroon Gulch where you found the quartz?" One of my boys asked.

"Someday we'll drive up to Maroon Lake and I'll point out the ledge from the new highway. You boys ought to climb up with rock hammer and drills and try some holes? Maybe if you shot away a couple of feet from the top, the quartz might be richer than the dickens—You know, that Navajo must have found something!"

The End

Rich wrote the preceding short story sometime in the years before his death in 1950. I was born a few years after his death, so I never got the chance to meet him, but knew his son, Robert (Uncle Bob to me) very well, as he married my grandmother's sister, Jean, and for about 10 years was my next-door neighbor in Woodbine, New Jersey. I remember many times his stories about the West, and his stories about prospecting for gold, silver, and uranium, as well as his stories about his dad, Rich Thomson. Later, after I moved to Glenwood Springs myself in 1972, (as Bob and Jean had done a few years earlier) I learned more about both prospecting and his father's prospecting days and verified some of the prospecting stories by examining several of the mining claims records contained within the Garfield County records building.... Daniel Parliman.

THE RENDEZVOUS AT WILD HORSE SPRING
BY RICH ROY THOMSON

This story takes place, just after October 13, 1896, in Western Colorado

Owen Braun was a wild horse trapper; the best among a group of daring and resourceful men who made their living at this exciting line of work in northwestern Colorado at about the turn of the century.

In the vast, sparsely settled regions extending from the valley of the Grand River (now called the Colorado River) north to the Lower White River, thence north to the Bear River, and on to the Wyoming line, Owen's fame as a horse trapper and trainer of wild horses had spread from camp to camp, ranch to ranch. It was said that his name was better known than that of the Governor, especially as you got further back from the railroads, into that wild back country.

In the section of the country between the lower White River and the Bear River, he had been operating for some years. Owen had built his summer camp cabin at Wild Horse Spring, far up near the headwaters of Wolf Creek and near the high hogback mountain separating the White and Bear watersheds. The spring, appropriately named through the fact that it had been a watering place for wild horses for centuries, as long as horses have existed after escaping first the Spanish, then the native Americans who lived around this isolated country. Primarily in this very section of Colorado, it would probably have been the Utes, although other tribes sometimes hunted this extreme northwest corner of Colorado that was mostly in the White River watershed. No one had ever fenced the spring; preventing stock from accessing its cool waters.

Even at the time of our story, wild horses would venture into the water during the night. No cattle came up this far from the rivers, and cowboys seldom rode this far back. Other wild horse men considered this Owen Braun's particular wild horse range, and except for the few horse buyers who knew its location, other visitors were few.

As for Owen Braun himself, rarely has a man been so widely talked of and so scarcely known. Even his best, or closest friends, when inquiring where he came from, received the one answer: "From up north".

There was no further answer. His questioners could assume "up north" meant Wyoming, Montana, or even the far reaches of British Columbia. Men did not, in those days, press the issue. A man's birthplace, or other private affairs, was his own business. His nearest neighbor, some twenty-five miles away over hard trails, did not understand his past any more than his casual acquaintances. All agreed he was a real horseman, modest, and "a mighty fine man".

While his daily life was anything but a quiet, inactive one, his contacts with the outside world were comparatively rare.

Owen was a man in his early thirties, a trifle over six feet in height, and of slender build. His sharply sloping shoulders further gave the impression of frailness at first glance, and in repose, he was not an impressive figure. Modeled much on the height and build of the many cowboys of the west, until one saw him in action and noted his eyes, there was little to show the dynamic power of the man. That he was a horseman such as they had never seen, was attested by the occasional cowboy or horse buyer visitors who had watched him working with horses. And work them he did. He sold no horse until the horse was thoroughly broken, at least to where any good horseman could ride or lead him out to the river. Unlike many trappers of wild horses, Owen sold no unbroken or worthless horses to buyers of stock for rendering plants, or others who dealt in "killer horses". He did not believe in this kind of ending for a horse, and to make sure that the worthless ones caught in his traps would not later be re-caught and sold as "killer horses", he used his branding iron (Bar B) on everything he caught.

The horse buyers with whom he did business, and who always came to his camp for the purpose, (Owen receiving no mail, nor sending out any) were men who wished to buy stock which would make top cow horses. Also, at that time polo ponies were then in demand at the polo field in Glenwood Springs, and in other western Colorado towns.

Wild mares, the suitable type, were often halter broke and led to Owen's big canyon pasture, where Owen released them with other mares and Owen's pick of the stallions he had captured. After a while, he released them back to the wild herds. He understood he might never catch her again, but he knew her colt would be a worthy prize for someone. Owen was in the horse business for the long haul.

It was only in a corral full of frantic wild horses that Braun showed at his best. He stepped inside, afoot, and, with a rope in hand, a single cast of a small loop, would snare the neck of the animal he wanted. With his high spiked boot heels sunk into the ground, he would "sit down on the rope". The ordinary roper expects to be jerked loose from his first stand, and if no snubbing post is available, jerked around roughly by the frantic and plunging horse. Not so Owen. With the rope around his hip and a strength never observed by the oldest cowhands, his frail appearing body became an anchor of spring steel. The terror-stricken bronco, plunging, bucking, and bawling with every ounce of strength, could not move the man at the other end of the rope, and finally choked down. With the litheness and speed of a mountain lion attacking a deer, Owen would reach the outstretched horse's head. With foot on neck, he'd grasp the fleshy upper lip of the animal, raise the nose upright and, with his free hand, jerk the noose from around the horse's neck. The noose then, by a single flick, was enlarged and thrown over the two front feet, jerked tight and in a single leap the man would stand a few feet away from the pawing front feet. As the horse struggled to get the front legs out ahead so that he could arise, Owen would make a sudden jerk on the rope, so timed that at each attempt, his raised head would again fall back to the ground. After a few moments of this punishment, the horse would quiet down for a moment and lie still. Owen could then throw a lariat of the rope around the upper hind leg, and with what looked like a continuous single operation, jerk the leg forward until it crossed the two front legs. Next, he would make several turns around all three and jerk tight with a half-hitch, and the horse was "tied down" for keeps.

With the single exception of general use of a snubbing post to use in choking down the wild horse, this was the procedure used by all horse breakers. Asked why he did not have a good snubbing post in his corrals, or traps, and save himself much hard work, he replied: "Well, my experience with wild horses is that they're liable to run into the post and cripple themselves. Lots of good ropes get broken, and I just can't stand to abuse a good rope that way. Besides, I like to work horses with my hands alone."

As mentioned above, many men could handle the work of tying down a bronco horse, maybe not so smoothly and quickly as Owen, but in much the same manner. It was only after he put the horse into a hackamore, his left foreleg doubled and tied with hoof against forearm and was up on his feet, that one saw the resulting difference. One old cowhand described it better and quicker than any words I might use. "He investigates the hosses eyes, and stares and stares—he softly whispers a few words and rubs the broncs nose. Then he slips his off-hack rein under the neck, reaches over, and gets it, he cheeks 'em and puts his finger in the near eye, jerks the piggin' string on foreleg loose, and straddles up on that horse and is ready to go afore the hosses foot hits the ground."

His horses buck as hard as with anyone, but he sat them as on a loping horse. After the first go-around, and the horse stopped for wind, he would order his watcher to lower the bars. He and the bronc would take to the open country. In half an hour he'd be riding back, his mount a half broke horse.

THE RENDEZVOUS
AT WILD HORSE SPRING

Such a man was Owen Braun and his way of life; as on this evening of
our story, he rode from the point where he had set out a couple of rope
snares on a horse trail some miles to the west of his ranch. He made
these snares with about thirty feet of five-eighths inch semi-soft twist
rope. In a section of trail which crosses through a heavy stand of oak
and choke-cherry brush, a three-foot open loop of the rope would be
suspended over the trail by horse tail hairs, the upper part of the loop
above the height of a running horses head, the lower part about three
feet from the ground. Owen then spread out from the circle of rope;
other horse hairs tied to the brush along the trail kept it in its circular
form and other horse hairs bound in place, a garland of twigs and green
leaves completely covering all the other parts. He tied the free end of
the rope near the top of several stout but springy oak or cherry brush
limbs, their flexibility preventing the breaking of rope, or a horse's neck
as the loop tightened around it. Of course, a rider had to be close on
the tails of the wild horses that might get snared, to prevent the choking
of the captured animal. Based on his experience, he could safely let the
snares set overnight, as the wild horses, through fear of the many
mountain lions in the area, would never travel a timbered or brush
covered trail during darkness. He planned to arise at daybreak and ride
out over the top country. If he could jump a bunch of wild horses, he
would try to spook them off toward trails leading to his pre-set horse
snares.

Several days before, Owen had sighted a beautiful golden yellow stallion
(a color phase extremely rare in those days) with a small bunch of mares.
Owen watched them through his field glasses long enough to note the
size and beauty of the stallion and had noted an unusual custom of the
horse. Instead of the mares leading out in front when the band was
traveling, as they did on a range they knew, the stallion always took the
lead. Owen figured the bunch had never been in the country before,
probably ran out of their native range by other trappers trying to catch
the golden colored stallion. As Owen rode into camp, his thoughts were
of far away. "What a horse the golden one would make for the girl"; he
thought and was determined to win her hand in the coming months.

As he unsaddled at the corral, it surprised him to see a lone horseman riding down the ridge toward his camp. The rider rode straight to Owen, who waited at the corral gate, and as he pulled his horse to a stop, the stranger said: "Howdy, Mister, are you fixed so you can put up me and my horse for the night?"

Owen did not like the appearance of the man, never-the-less, politely asked him to "get down" and turn his horse into the small pasture adjoining the corral.

As the two men ate their supper a short time later, the stranger talked freely without prompting by his host. He claimed to be a "Rep" for the UCC (The Utah Cattle Company), a large outfit running stock in Utah and north-western Colorado. He had been on the ride with the Two-Bar at their Wagon line camp, when he had received a letter telling of sickness in his family out in Utah and leaving his bed and remuda with the Two-Bar outfit, had started on what he thought was a shortcut along the Bear-White River divide. He could see the cabin from the ridge top, and he had ridden down to get trail directions and to see if he could hang up for the night.

Owen listened in silence and wondered why the man had not brought his bed horse and bed along, as was the common custom of those traveling across the country. He did not mention this, but, as according to the code, any man's affairs were his own.

The stranger, the same height as Owen, was of much heavier build and in his early forties. Dressed in the typical clothing of the cowboys, Owen had no reason to believe he was other than what he claimed to be. Apart from his facial characteristics, he might have been any of the several thousand cowboys who worked in western Colorado. The face was unfamiliar to that of anyone whom Owen had met. Most of the men one met in the back country of that period were of unblemished skin, frank, open countenance, and with eyes that looked square into yours. Even though they were tough, some with pasts they dared not disclose, and some you knew were lovable scoundrels, all prided themselves in a warm, firm handshake and the ability to look the world in the eye.

Low browed, heavy black eyebrows, bushy and untrained to an animal appearance, shaded a pair of dark eyes which never moved as a normal person would do, but darted from here to there in a search for something they could not find.

His inquiries as to the trails which lead into Utah, coupled with Owen's account of his wild horse range, occupied the after-supper hour. Owen noting that his visitor appeared tired, fixed up the upper bunk for him and they retired early.

Owen was unaccustomed to visitors and the conversation of the evening caused Owen's sleep to be fitful and disturbed. He awoke several times. His guest's sleep, while that of an exhausted man, seemed somewhat troubled with dreams. Owen listened intently to his muttering and broken sentences. Apparently, he was engaged in a heated conversation with a "Shorty" and a "Bill", and with several references to "the bank". This meant little to Owen. He had met dozens of men known as Shorty or Bill, and "the bank" was just one of those places where the "Pumpkin Bellies" of the farms went to borrow money during slack crop years. With little thought to his guest's muttered talk, he finally fell asleep and did not awaken until daylight. His guest arose shortly after, and while Owen was cooking the breakfast of buck loin steak, gravy, biscuits, and coffee, took down his carbine from the wooden pegs where he had placed it the night before.

The gun, a twenty-inch round barrel Winchester, and (back then), a comparatively new 30-30 caliber, was much the same as Owen's. Most men owned these short saddle guns—handy arms for killing buckskin (deer) when they needed meat, or to shoot lion, bear, or grey wolves that sometimes preyed upon their stock. Few cowboys made a practice of carrying them upon the roundups—there was too much danger of losing them from the saddle scabbards when riding circle in the heavy brush and most of the boys left them at the home ranch.

The visitor examined the gun carefully, ejected the shells from the magazine, and reloaded again. He then placed it on the wall pegs as Owen announced that breakfast was ready.

As his guest sat down to eat, Owen noticed that his six shooter was in its scabbard. While all men in the hills carried a belt gun as a matter of course while outside, always having the time worn expression of the old timers in mind, "Maybe you'll never need it, but when you do, you'll need it bad." It was a common courtesy, just as removing one's Stetson hat, to hang up the six-shooter on a nail alongside one's hat, when indoors.

Following a hearty breakfast, the guest calmly announced, "If you don't mind, I think I will stay here another day and rest my horse some more."

Owen nodded a pleasant assent. While he had a distinct disliking for the man, the appearance of his horse, head down, gaunt, flanked, and dull eyed as he stood inside the pasture fence, helped to make the invitation to stay more agreeable. To Owen's practiced eye, the horse was badly "bed rocked", and needed rest.

Owen caught up his top horse for the day's ride, a big leggy sorrel gelding, carrying on his father's side the royal blood of an imported English thoroughbred. The Two-Bar outfit on the Bear River had had this young stallion brought in and placed on one of their ranches. But that stallion had escaped from his box stall one day, jumped the low ranch fences and taken off to the hills, where he had joined a bunch of wild horses. The memory of his box stall, regular oat, and bran mash feeding, was soon forgotten in his love of freedom and the wild mares with which he ran. The Two-Bars put a half dozen riders out after him, and they trailed him hard for three weeks, finally getting him alone, as the mares played out and deserted the band, one by one. They finally lost his tracks at a point where they led into the Bear River and could never pick them up again. Some of the Two-Bar hands presumed he deliberately took to the river and drowned, rather than risk capture. At least that was the story among the old hands for many years afterward.

Owen knew differently, however. Some six years back, he had run into this horse as he climbed a long ridge leading south from the Bear. Alone, sore-footed, exhausted, and gaunt as a rail. Owen did not know the story of the Two Bar stallion. He knew horses, though. Despite the stallion's poor condition, he readily recognized at a distance the horse for what he was. Owen Dismounted and leaving his saddle horse, he slowly approached the horse with his inverted hat in outstretched hand, moving it gently and cooing a low voice horse lullaby. The stallion stood still and watched the approaching man. This was not one of the loud swearing, mounted wild men who had been dashing at him with a swinging lariat, but one of his own kind from across the sea, the kind who "cooed," and brought oats to him in his hat when he was a colt. He whinnied and took a few steps forward, stepped and snorted; Owen remained quiet. The horse advanced a few more steps, and paused in indecision, and Owen slowly walked up to its head. The stallion nosed the hat but found no oats. A hand was gently stroking his face in a way he liked, while Owen slipped the other one over his neck. With the piggin string he carried around his waist, Owen rigged a short lead rope and led the stallion back to his saddle horse. Placing his lariat on the stallion, Owen made a hackamore and led him back to camp. There he examined him carefully and found him slick, no sign of a brand marking his satiny hide. On the front side of his left front hoof, near the ground line and in a few months to be worn completely away, were four or five numbers burned lightly into the shell. Owen recalled he had read of the English custom of burning the horse's pedigree numbers on the hoof, a hot iron on the skin never being used.

Owen was not worried at all as to the point of ownership of the horse he had captured so easily. Under the unwritten law of the range, the horse was slick, and his so long as he kept possession. Under the seldom used Colorado state law, whether branded or unbranded, the former owner could recover the horse if he could prove legal ownership. In either case, he felt no responsibility other than to make sure the horse was properly fed and water; and taken care of for the present.

A few miles west of Owen's cabin was a box canyon of several miles long, inaccessible rock walls on either side, and blocked at its upper end by cliffs. At the lower end of the box, Owen had, by much labor, built a stout Cedar palisade fence across from cliff to cliff, with a heavy pole gate in the center. At one place, a year-long spring of good water came out and its water ran down the draw for a hundred yards before sinking in the sand. The canyon was filled with a rank growth of grass and browse plants, and after fencing, formed a pasture where horses could be kept throughout the year if necessary. Owen placed the stallion in with a bunch of picked mares he had captured and broken during the summer.

From one of these mares, a short, coupled bay, Owen figured was of at least half Morgan breeding, he raised a colt sired by the Two-Bar horse. At three, this colt was such an animal seldom seen in the country, and under Owens careful breaking and training was the best wild horse mount he had ever seen. Such a horse was "The Duke", so named from his sire's noble ancestry, and the horse caught up to ride that day.

The visitor eyed him with undisguised admiration, and with a show of studied casualness, announced: "Young feller, I'll give you two hundred dollars for that pony". Now ordinarily cowboys did not run around with that kind of money, neither did they give an unheard-of price of two hundred dollars, when the best cow horses in the country could be bought for fifty or sixty dollars, Owen thought of this, then shook his head: "No, I can't let him go. In my business he is the best horse I know, and I just can't sell him". He turned and rode away, calling back as an afterthought: "I might not get back until late. If you look under my bunk, you'll find the meat rolled in a tarp. Also, the spuds are there too. Everything else is in the cupboards".

The stranger gazed steadily as he rode away, his beady eyes for once fixed intently on The Duke.

Owen encountered no luck in capturing or seeing any wild horses that day. He had ridden far and wide down the hogback country. When he passed his two snares in the late evening, he left them hanging open. Nothing would be liable to get into them during the night, he thought, and possibly he might jump a bunch early in the morning that he could run that way. He rode on into camp at dark.

His guest had prepared supper, and everything seemed alright as they finished the meal and washed up the dishes. Owen noticed the man had taken his rifle down from the wall pegs, and the gun stood against the wall near the door. His guest may have seen him eying the gun, or possibly for other reasons, advanced the information that he thought he saw a lion out in the cedars. He had taken the gun down in the hope of a shot at the big cat.

The men retired early and slept soundly. Owen slept well. He never knew when he retired what was in his guest's mind and did not know until many hours later.

His guest's behavior changed before daybreak, when he lay in his bunk and listened to Owen's deep and regular snoring. He slid quietly down off the foot of his bunk and reached the floor. In stocking feet, he carefully crept across the dirt floor to the wood box and groped until his hand closed over a heavy two-inch piece of partly seasoned jock oak, which had been cut a bit too long for the stove firebox and had been laid aside.

Walking back to the bunks, he ignited a bunch of matches in his left hand. As the sudden bright flame lit up Owen's bed, he awoke and turned over. The visitor uttered a curse and brought the heavy oak club down with a crushing force on Owen's head. His body stretched out rigidly, his eyelids fluttered slightly, and he lay quiet.

The man saw this before his matches burned out. He saw Owen's six shooter hanging on a nail near the head of the bunk and snatched it up. As the matches burned out, he lit others, then as the body before him showed no movement, he stepped to the table and lit the kerosene lamp. With Owen's pistol in his left hand and the oak stick in the right, he approached the bed again. His first thought was to batter the helpless man's head into a pulp, to make sure his work was complete. His thoughts raced to his plans for escape, riding away on his victim's wonderful horse. A disquieting thought came to mind. Had Owen Braun told him to take the right, or was it the left fork of the trail? One led into the country where there were several ranches and cow camps, the other through isolated regions where he probably would never see a man until he was well into Utah. The annoying thought grew to a panic. He stepped to the bed and turned Owen's body onto its back. The right eye had swollen completely shut. A blood soaked and swollen welt extended back along the side of the head. The stranger picked up an arm and felt for the pulse and noted with relief that the heart was still beating. He smiled cruelly. "Hopefully he will live long enough to tell me the correct trail again", he said aloud, then rushed outside the cabin. In a matter of seconds, he was back again with Owen's lariat. Looping a small noose over the battered and bleeding head of the unconscious man, he drew it until there was no play of the rope around the neck. He then wrapped the rope from the neck twice around the body and legs in such a manner that any struggles of this bound man would pull the neck rope tight and choke its victim. This inhuman method of tying up prisoners had at one time been a common practice of some outlaw Indians, and the man apparently comprehended its use well. He finished up by tying the feet securely to the heavy pole at the foot of the bunk, then ran the rope forward and tied Owen's hands to the pole forming at the front end of the bunk.

He surveyed his work with satisfaction, and as it appeared there was no hope of Owen releasing himself, he left the cabin.

The Duke was a well-trained horse, and the man had no trouble in catching him. He walked to the corral and saddled up, then returned to the cabin.

Owen had regained consciousness during the stranger's absence, and in a few seconds realized the position he was in, the neck rope tightening up at his first attempt to turn and arise from the bed.

He heard the approaching sound of the horse as the stranger led him to the cabin door. Owen next recognized a whinny from the Duke as the horse was left ground-tied nearby.

Owen's first thought was of the loss of his horse, this changing to a chilling fear as he noted the stranger's face when he entered. No longer just a mean vicious looking man, his features no longer tried to mask their brutality.

Owen was not a coward by any measure men ordinarily used, but he involuntarily held his breath at the possibilities which lay before him.

The man saw Owen was conscious and lost no time in asking what he wanted to know. Owen gave a frank and truthful description of the trails to the west as far as he knew them, the man taking notes in his pocket tally book. As he completed his questioning, he pocketed his tally book and, reaching down again, picked up the blood-stained piece of oak. Owen had turned his head slightly and, with his uninjured eye, saw the man's intentions. He did not cry out; he made no move, there was nothing he could do. His thoughts raced as a whirlwind, but with no answer. Through the open door, a shaft of sunlight fell across the bed, his open eye being in its path. He gazed at the advancing man, but his lips did not move. The stranger looked into the eye of the helpless man, turned his eyes away, and looked again. Owen had looked into the eyes of a thousand horses, horses so wild that only he could control them. He had willed in his mind that they do as he wished; he knew not why - he knew they obeyed his wishes. As the man closed in with an up-raised club, Owen's eye again caught those of his assailant and held them despite his futile attempt to look away. He faltered and stopped, cursed, and dropped the club to the floor - "D____n you, I never could kill a man when he was down," he gasped and turned toward the door. Owen's breath returned, his muscles relaxed, and he closed his eye for an instant. He saw the man start for the door and as he reached it, raised his hand up and pulled Owen's prize Winchester down from its pegs. Owen's breath stopped again as the man looked toward him. "Was he to die from his own gun?" he thought.

The man stepped outside, and Owen heard the crash as the stranger struck the Winchester again and again against a rock. The man stepped inside again and eyed the helpless man. "You sure got plenty of nerve, young fellow, and I could use you if you were the useable kind, but you're not." He turned and filled his pockets with biscuits and meat left from the evening meal, walked to the open door with Owen's field glasses, looked over the country within sight of the cabin. Pulling a chair to the open door, from where he could see a considerable distance along several trails leading into the camp, the man started talking. "It won't make much difference to you, young feller, but while I'm waiting for that horse to eat his nose bag of oats, I'm going to tell you a little story."

He went on with a tale, the complete wording of which Owen could never remember. It is not at all strange the exact words were forgotten, because it came to Owen with a sickening realization that no man in his right mind would tell such a story to even a helpless captive and take the chance of leaving that man alive: To repeat it in a court sometime, or to shoot him down on sight, it did not add up correctly. Owen listened. There was nothing else he could do.

Shorty, Bill, Bill's young son, and the stranger had ridden up the White River from Utah, and about where the state line crossed into Colorado had taken to the high country between the White River and the Bear River to avoid meeting people, and to look up their route for a return trip. Shorty had at one time punched cows for the old K outfit, and knew the general lay of the country. They had passed through near Owen's camp and had noted the several splendid horses in Owen's pasture. "We figured we might rendezvous here for a few days if everything turned out right. Shorty wanted to wait until you came back to camp that evening and dry gulch you, but I figured we might use you later." The man continued. The four reached Strawberry Creek and camped in a heavy oak thicket some eight or ten miles out of Meeker, the County seat, and center of a rich ranching and cattle country. Riding into Meeker, they had looked over the town carefully. There was only one bank in town, and it looked like a perfect setup for several smart men of nerve, and they figured they could lift its funds with little trouble. After a few days of looking over the layout, the brains decided as to the day and hour the bank holdup would take place.

The leader returned to their Strawberry Creek camp and prepared for the next morning's work. All the pack saddles, camp equipment, and beds were burned that night. The next morning, only the leader and four horses remained at their camp. At near the hour arranged for the bank holdup, the leader, who identified himself as Owen's "visitor", climbed to the top of a knoll near camp, where he could look down country toward Meeker for several hours. At the designated hour, he had heard heavy gun fire toward Meeker. This had not been a part of the plans at all. A quick holdup of the bank employees, scooping all the money into a grain bag, herding those in the bank into the vault and locking them in. It had appeared simple. Strolling out and mounting their horses at the nearby hitching rack and loping out of town. The stranger cursed fiercely. "The stupid fools, the stupid fools", he repeated over and over. He had waited a few minutes, then ran back down to camp. "They'll have a posse right on their tails". It's their funeral. He mounted and took off through the rough country on the predetermined escape route. The man finished in a tirade of curses against his former companions and turned toward the door. Owen asked, "What are you going to do about me?" The man smiled evilly. "I'll leave you tied and maybe some cowboy will come along and turn you loose. They say you are a wonder with a rope. Maybe you can figure out a way to untie your own rope." With this, the man left the cabin.

Owen heard the man stirring around outside the closed cabin door. The "stranger" threw something against it. Again, he heard the same sound and recognized it as an armful of stove firewood from his wood supply, and the realization of what the man was about to do struck him at the same instant. He uttered a moan of despair. No cry to the man outside. He knew this to be hopeless. Utter despair was the certainty the outlaw leader would cause him to be roasted alive, in the only home he knew, and one he loved so well.

The galloping hoofs of his horse came to his ears before he heard the crackling of flames and smelled the pungent cedar and pinion smoke.

He strained at the ropes binding his hands and feet, body rigid to prevent pull on the rope around his neck. His head was aching with an unbearable pain, the rope gave not an inch; the man had tied down too many steers not to know his job. Owen's heart raced, the blood flowing into the welt on his head until it appeared it would break through in a stream, and he lapsed into merciful unconsciousness.

The light dry wood placed against the outside of the door burned fiercely, flames reaching nearly to the eaves of the cabin. Smoke crept through the cracks and filled the interior of the cabin; Owen coughed a few times and lay still.

The cabin door was of rough pine boards, and as the flames increased, they caught and ate their way along its edges at each side.

Now when Owen had built the cabin, he had packed in the door boards from the little general store at Rangely, about 60 miles west of Meeker. The store had no hinges in stock, so Owen, rather than wait until he could get the steel type hinges, had cut some leather ones from an old pack saddle rigging, as was quite a common practice in those days.

As the flames reached the lower hinge and caught, dry as tinder, it burned through in less than a minute. The door fell partly inside and hung at an angle. The upper hinge caught and burned through, and the door fell inside with a crash, given the weight of burning and unburnt wood leaning against it.

The practice of those building a cabin was similar as of the present day, convenience was one of the first thoughts. In Owen's cabin, the bench holding the water bucket and wash basin were placed just inside, and to one side of the door. On this morning the several-gallon pail was practically full, and as the door fell, it struck the corner of the bench. The pail and contents fell onto the door, water spread and over time, extinguished most of the flames. The wood outside burned out completely without igniting the heavy logs on each side of the door.

It was late afternoon before the quiet figure on the bed stirred. As he regained consciousness, Owen did not realize at first his situation. With head bursting in pain, his body burning with fever, lungs still containing too much smoke-filled air, he was confused. Until the ropes tightened, and then he remembered his last conscious moments. He coughed, felt the clutch of the rope around his neck, and recollection came with a rush. Owen sniffed the air and detected no current smoke. He turned his head slightly and could see no sign of the fire still burning. He realized it had gone out and breathed a sigh of short-lived relief.

The hopelessness of his condition came back over him, and he knew that there might not be a visitor to his camp for weeks, and he thought of the days and nights without water. The mental anguish at the thought of dying like an animal in a trap — Suddenly the last words of the would-be murderer came to his troubled mind — "They say you are a wonder with a rope", He knew this was true, and the idea brought back instantly a return of Owen's normal and practical, clear thinking, his methodical way of step-by-step thinking, surmounting the difficulties before him. He even thought of an old story so often told around the cow camps: of how a roundup boss inquired of the horse-wrangler, how and where he had found the lost remuda of horses. "Where did you find em, Bill?" and the wranglers reply in cowboy jargon "I just thought iffen I was a hoss, whar would I go? So thar I went, and thar they war." Owen did not think of the humor in the story. His thoughts were of the deadly serious prospect before him.

Owen thought first of the rope, and the half hitches binding his hands and feet to the poles at each end of the bed. He knew there was no weakness of the rope; Owen had tried it out too many times. He understood the half hitches around the poles, and his limbs could not be loosened. His thoughts turned to the poles to which he was bound. He remembered building the bunk from stout peeled aspen poles, built to last. There was no possibility that either the front or foot poles could be broken, no matter the level of stress that might be placed upon them by the ropes.

The pole at the foot of the bunk was nailed to the upright posts from the outside, the pole at the front was nailed to the uprights from the front, or bunk side, Owen gave a start - his pulse quickened, as it came to him. The recollection that when he had built the bunks, he had just about ran out of nails. He remembered that the front pole had been toe nailed into place with just a couple of small nails at each end, the heavy spikes having all been previously used.

He lay for some minutes, planning each step carefully, then opened his good eye and raised his head ever so slightly.

The rope leading from the neck loop led around his body, thence around the upper part of his legs, and out between his knees to the pole, at the foot of the bed.

He raised his knees slightly until he felt the hard, twisted lariat between them. Clinching the legs until he pressed the rope tightly between the hard, bony knee structure, Owen slowly contracted the muscles of his upper arms and shoulders, his body rigid, and pulled with all his strength. A faint squeak caught his ear as the nails loosened at the outside the end of the pole. It pulled free and struck the top of his head. He lifted his numbed arms and raised the pole over his face and onto his breast. He squirmed his body toward the foot of the bunk to relieve the strain on the tightened neck loop, then lay quietly for a moment in the joy of victory, for no longer did he have a doubt as to his eventual release.

As his arms lay before him, his fingers were practically numb. He moved the arms close to the pole and the spring of the hard twist loosened the half hitches on his wrists slightly. Owen raised the pole into the air as far as he could reach, brought them back down, and repeated the movement time after time. He kept his fingers moving as fast as he could until finally circulation was better and feeling returned to the hands. With fingers working slowly but surely, he advanced the triple half hitches on the pole toward its end, only to find that he could not reach far enough to get the hitches off the end of the pole. Patiently, he worked them back to the center, then by lifting the pole up and down for some time, the light nails at its inside end loosened and the end fell into the bunk. He rested for a moment. The torment of thirst, burning fever and throbbing head spurred him on. Fingering the half hitches toward the inside-end of the pole this time, he soon worked them to the very end and over the short nail ends, and the pole finally tumbled free on to the cabin floor.

"Two half hitches will hold the Devil," had been the saying of cowboys since the beginning of time. They will do just this, providing they are encircling something solid. Remove the object as their clinging coils encircle, and they become little harmless snarls in a rope. Owen shook them loose, and with a section held fast in his teeth, soon worked the hitches off his wrists. Extending his arms against the head of the bunk, he pushed his body back toward the foot, gained a little slack, and pulled the noose over his head. To raise up and release his feet was only a few seconds' job, and he lowered his legs to the cabin floor. Trying to walk, his feet and ankles refused to function, and he fell to his knees. His lower legs and feet were numb with the thousands of stinging needles and numbness as the blood began circulating freely once again. It took a couple of minutes for the numbness to recede, although not yet normal.

Crawling to the stove, he clutched the coffeepot by the rim and drank the cold black and bitter coffee right down to the grounds. He crawled to the nearest chair and pulled his body upon it. Owen Braun continued rubbing and massage for several minutes, which finally brought a return of normal circulation, and he could finally begin walking.

For the next two days, Owen spent his time between the spring and the cabin. The only medicine he had in camp, the only one in fact that he had ever felt necessary for camp use, was table salt.

Alternate applications of hot saltwater compresses and ice-cold spring water to his injured eye and head area worked wonders, and on the morning of the third day he was much his usual self.

Shortly after he had freed himself, he had noticed the bed-rocked horse belonging to the self-styled bank robber, standing just inside the open gate of the pasture. The other two horses he had previously had there were missing, either driven out by his visitor or they had drifted out later.

Owen caught the horse and saddled up, with the intention of riding him to his pasture where he had other broke horses. The mount, apparently a young and sound horse, proved so still and wind broken that Owen doubted whether he could carry him across the rough canyon short-cut trail to the pasture. He decided against trying it and took the longer but smoother going trail leading up on to the hog-back. Reaching the top, he thought of the snares he had left open several evenings before. Worried with the thought that some horse might have been snared and choked himself to death, he turned off on the trail leading down to the snares.

Entering the patch of heavy oak and chokecherry brush where the snares had been left, Owen was unprepared for the sudden snort and whirl of his horse. He had been ducking the overhanging brush, and until his horse shied and whirled, had noticed nothing unusual. Now, as he turned and looked down the trail, he saw a snare rope stretched tightly across before him. At the end and slightly to one side, lay the body of a man. The loop of the snare encircled his neck, his bluish face looking toward the sky, his eyes bulging out of the open lids. Owen sprang from his horse and ran to the body, gave one look at the bloated features, and recognized them as those of his late visitor.

The picture of what had happened came clearly to Owen: The man spurring his horse at a hard lope along the trail, the loop of snare somehow missing the horse's head and encircling that of the man.

Owen stooped to remove the rope from the body of the dead man, when he was startled by the familiar whinny of a horse. There, as he looked down the trail a few yards, stood "The Duke", a loose noose around his neck. Other than being very thin and gaunt, he appeared to be unharmed.

By some stroke of fate, the horse's head had missed the first snare and caught its rider. Owen always thought about this for years afterward. He supposed it happened because The Duke had seen him put up the snares and knowing the effects of a snare from his younger days, when Owen had caught him several times that way in the pasture, had deliberately ducked under the first snare. His idea was that when the man was jerked from The Duke's back, he had become rattled and forgotten the second snare. When it pulled tight on his shoulders, Duke had come to a sliding stop without over-tightening the loop.

Why had the stranger not taken the correct trail, the one without the snares? Owen could think of no reason unless the stranger just did not trust him. Perhaps thinking a man about to die would not be truthful?

Owen removed the loop, noting that the man's neck had been broken. "Never knew what hit him," thought Owen, as he gazed down at the body. Mixed emotions swept through him. Neither pity nor horror being a part. His life had been difficult, and in an unforgiving country. He had been close to death many times, had seen it strike swiftly and unexpectedly, several times against his close friends.

As I have said before, Owen was a practical man, and he accepted the accidental death of the man by his snare, as a justified and well-deserved act of providence, and of little further consideration. His emotions were of a distinct character, the question of what he should do next? It would require much thought, and he would have to sit down and figure it out in his own methodical way. He selected a comfortable, mostly flat rock nearby and prepared to go over the whole situation.

If he did the right thing under custom and the laws of the state of Colorado, there would be many things for him to do.

First, he would have to go to the big pasture and leave The Duke, who needed food and water badly. He would catch up a couple of broke horses and return to camp. Then he would have to return to the man's body with a sack of salt to use in preventing further decay, and to kill the flies and worms. Next, it would have to be bound up tightly in a tarp brought from camp, to prevent further decay and attacks from the magpies. The step next required the shoeing of a horse for the long day's ride into Meeker, to notify the sheriff and coroner. Next day would be the long ride back to camp and to the body. The sheriff and coroner would probably insist that the remains be brought into Meeker for an inquest. That would require his shoeing of a packhorse, and the unpleasant long day taken up by packing the stinking body at least to the nearest road. Next would come the inquest and innumerable embarrassing questions to answer before a large crowd. Then, at last, another full day's ride back to camp, nearly a week used up, and all for what?

The picture did not add up right. What if the man's story of an attempted holdup of the bank was all a lie? What if some people would not believe his story of the attempted murder, and instead later might spread the tale that Owen had deliberately chased a rival horse trapper into the snare? Owen almost moaned as he thought of the possibilities ahead.

Owen turned the situation around to another viewpoint. No one knew the dead man had ever been to his camp. No one knew his body lay here in the thicket, no one would ever know these things. What if he simply dragged the body to the sink hole a hundred yards down the mountainside and dropped it down into the bowels of the earth? One time, a horse had died not too far from here, struck by lightning during a thunderstorm. To avoid the attraction of vultures and other eaters of carrion, Owen had cut the horse's body into pieces and dragged them with his rope and horse to the sinkhole. The hole was deep, one character of nature found in limestone formations, common in places like this. An old water course probably leading to unknown depths. He recalled listening for a minute or more at the rumble of the horse's remains, as they fell and rolled deeper and deeper into the earth.

The picture became clearer and more logical, only he would ever see, or know, and he was not a man to talk of his past. A little inborn sense of duty to custom and law troubled him for a moment, then his thoughts turned to a disquieting channel. Perhaps the man had a mother? Would the persistent sheriff learn the identity of the "stranger?" Is it possible the monthly newspapers would spread the story of his misdeeds throughout the land, and the mother read of it? Did he have a vengeful brother?

Owen's eyes filled with unaccustomed tears that burned as they crept down his cheek. This last thought was too much, and Owen was still grieving at its consequences as he prepared to attend to the duty before him. He lifted his own six shooter from the man's belt holster and placed it back into his own. He looped his lariat over the booted feet and dragged the body with his horse down to the nearby sink hole and released it over the edge. As it fell, Owen repeated a little brief prayer, the only one he had ever learned. He unconsciously spoke his afterthought aloud. "I guess he needs all the blessing he can get." As he rode back to the trail, he saw the man's heavy leather wallet lying in the grass, where it had fallen from the body. Owen got off and picked it up. For an instant he thought of opening it to see if the man's name might be learned, then thought better of the idea. He walked back to the sinkhole and threw it in. "I want none of another man's property," and he returned to the trail.

Owen removed the stranger's saddle, bridle, and blanket from The Duke. Owen glanced at the saddle carbine in the scabbard and started to carry it with the saddle to the sinkhole. He then thought of his own carbine lying in the rocks near the cabin, the stock battered off; the action battered and ruined, the barrel bent beyond repair. Pulling the carbine from the scabbard, he noted it was nearly exactly like his own had been, except for a dozen deep notches cut into the comb of the stock. He slipped it into his own scabbard with the non-spoken thought that a trade was a trade, fair in any man's country. After disposing of the saddle and bridle, he thought of bringing the stranger's horse to the sinkhole, shooting and rolling him in after his master. This idea was quickly discarded. "I'll take a chance and let the poor devil live out his life with the wild ones," and as he passed a spring shortly afterwards, simply turned him loose.

Some three weeks later, Owen returned to his camp one evening and was greeted at his cabin door by the Rio Blanco County sheriff and his deputy. Owen knew both men slightly, and although their greeting was open and cordial, he had many misgivings. The sheriff wanted to know if they could stop with him overnight, and Owen gave his usual gracious invitation to turn the horses in and make themselves at home.

While his host was cooking supper, the sheriff asked: "Owen, have you been seeing any strangers around here this summer, and have you been here all the time for the last month?" Owen turned, the light from the lamp falling full in his face, his eyes peering evenly and steadily into those of the sheriff. "Well, no, sheriff. You know there are mighty few visitors up here except the horse buyers who come in the fall. I haven't been out since I was out for grub about six weeks ago. It gets kind of lonesome sometimes." He then turned and took out the biscuits and placed them on the back of the stove. "I've got to get a little fresh water to settle the coffee, then we'll be ready to eat." He picked up the water pail and left for the spring.

The sheriff leaned across the table and whispered to his deputy,

"I was afraid this young fellow might be mixed up in it, but no man can look me in the eye and lie to me without me knowing it. I have been sheriff here since they formed the county in 1889." He sat back with a relieved sigh and continued aloud. "I guess there's no use looking further west. I'll bet if a strange jack rabbit ever went through these parts, he would know it."

As they ate supper, the sheriff told his story. "You know, they robbed the bank at Meeker three weeks ago. The three robbers were all killed, and we thought we had them all. Day before yesterday, Sam Weir, a cowman from down on the White River, was riding up on Strawberry Creek. In an oak thicket, he came into an old camp and found three horses tied up in the brush. Two had died, the third still alive, but in real bad shape. All the beds and camp outfit, grub and pack saddles had been burned up, and we figured the horses had been left there as relay stock for the escaping bank robbers. There was one queer thing, however. Near the three horses, we found there was a place where a fourth horse had been tied up. Also, in the dead oak leaves in the thicket, we found where four beds had been laid out. It looks like one man might have been left with the fresh horses and pulled out when his pardners failed to show up. We thought we had better scout around a few days and see if we could get a line on this missing man."

Owen had sat patiently through the sheriff's account of the attempted robbery. He was much interested in the minor details and questioned the sheriff occasionally. His frank, honest eyes were those of an innocent and simple man, and such he was, according to his code.

Several Generations Later

In Meeker today, some of the old, old timers talk of the town's one and only bank robbery. Some say the man that got away from the Strawberry camp might have been Butch Cassidy, Tom Horn, or one of many others. None are sure who it was, but some are certain there was a fourth man.

"But what's the story of that old, notched carbine in the gun rack, Dad?"

"Not much to tell, boys. An old friend gave it to me, along with the story I just told you."

October 13, 2021 was the 125th anniversary of the robbery at the Bank of Meeker. The townspeople acquitted themselves very well that day in 1896. Having killed all three of the known perpetrators, the townspeople successfully defended their bank, and their money in that bank.

There are still rumors that perhaps one or more "junior" members of the Butch Cassidy gang were involved in the robbery and that perhaps not all the gang were killed that day. There had been other Cassidy members involved in other known Colorado robberies, around that same timeframe, and after. Those of us who know the nearby Flattops and its surrounding wilderness know that there are many sinkholes and caves scattered throughout the area. Secrets can still be kept.

The following is a non-fictional story which was written around 1949, after the 1948 Thomson led Trail Ride, part of the Wilderness Trail rides which took place starting in 1933, sponsored by the American Forestry Association throughout the United States. For privacy reasons, Rich chose to use pseudonyms for most of the guest's names.

THE LAST ROUND UP
BY RICH ROY THOMSON

No, the "Last Roundup" title here is not referring to the well-known, popular western song of that same title, nor of the last big cattle round-up held in the West. Of considerably more importance and interest to the fifty-eight people who had an active part in it, my story is of our 1948 big Wilderness Trail Ride in the rugged mountains of western Colorado.

Now there are trail rides, and there are TRAIL RIDES. The first might mean a half-dozen eastern dudes and their guide, riding horseback up a wide trail some ten miles into the mountains, cooking their dinner over a campfire, and returning in the shank of the evening to the modern conveniences of a dude ranch or resort hotel. Other TRAIL RIDES, the kind we will deal with in this article, are horses of a far original color and size, as you will readily see.

Our "spread", not a western cattle outfit, with which the above term is commonly used, is never-the-less one of the largest spreads in the United States. We do not have cattle on a thousand hills—we do, however, have dudes (Trail Riders, if you please, in their presence) from forty-eight states, and quite a few strays from across the big pond.

To start at the beginning, back in 1933, the American Forestry Association, of Washington D.C., decided it would be a wonderful thing if nature loving people throughout the nation could have a satisfactory means of seeing the wonders of the wild, unsettled, rugged and altogether beautiful regions not reached by roads or railroads. The lack of any existing sleeping or eating accommodations in these areas meant, of course, that they would have to be covered on horseback, and all living facilities carried along by pack horses.

With these objectives in mind, the Association started a program sponsoring such pack trips on a non-profit basis in order that people of little experience could join an organized party and make a two-week trip in safety and comfort at a minimum cost. Since 1933, they have enlarged the program to where trips are made in seven western states and in the Great Smoky Mountains of North Carolina. To distinguish their trips from the hodgepodge of other unorganized rides, they have designated them as "The Trail Riders of the Wilderness".

In 1938, we were given the contract to handle the pioneer ride in the Colorado Rockies, and since that time until the late 1940s, have handled the greatest number of their expeditions in the West, and the largest parties in terms of numbers.

Our oldest son, Jim (R. James Thomson), at the time home from college on vacation, was assigned the job of covering and logging the proposed route of the pioneer "Trail Ride of the Wilderness" in Colorado. With different rangers assigned by the Forest Service to meet him at designated points and accompanying him through their districts, he covered the trip, which ordinarily takes two weeks for a Trail Ride party to accomplish, in four and one-half days. This does not mean that it was a four and one-half-day ride. His diary, showing prospective camp sites, desirable because of water, shelter, and feed, selected evidently with watch in hand, is one of my prized possessions as an example of speed and efficiency. From the daylight hours of four a.m. to the dusk at 8 p.m., Traveler and Jake, two of our top trail horses, with the speed of Pegasus, apparently flew from range to range.

Following several smaller expeditions which the Thomson Horse Haven (HH) Outfit had just completed in the White River Flat Top wilderness area during July 1948, there were feverish and super-hurtling events at our place near the small resort town of Glenwood Springs.

Cowboy wranglers moving horses from place to place, shoeing horses, camp men repairing tents, packing food, supplies, and equipment, and the hundreds of other preparatory chores.

At the end of a long and "get-the-job-done day", Pearl Ellis Thomson (Tommy), my better half, and Robert W. Thomson (Bob), our youngest son (age 28 in 1948), got together for our final pow-wow. (Jim was now in business for himself elsewhere in August,1948). "We've got 102 good trail horses shod, a fine crew of help, and everything is ready to start tomorrow."

In the organization of an expedition into the wilderness, from our viewpoint, the matter of lining up sufficient and a suitable type of horses is of first importance. Depending on the size of the party, from seventy-five to over a hundred head of horses must be gathered and shod up with full calked shoes.

I speak of "gathered" lightly, as though it might be a simple procedure, such as horse shoeing. However, it is not at all simple. Horses which Trail Riders are to ride on the trip must be "fool proof", or spoken within the hearing of inexperienced riders, "dude proof". They must be gentle and forbearing to the point of angelic and placid fortitude—to submit, without surprise or protest, to any strange situation in which their riders may place them. Cameras dangling low from the rear strings of their saddles, whacking them in the flank at each step, slickers half tied on the saddle and riding partly under the tail, as well as saddles slipped upon top of their withers, or back on the loins, all these are only a few of the indignities they must bear; withal they must be surefooted, intelligent, and "quite peppy".

To insure having the right kind, we carry over each winter about forty head of our own picked horses. To get the balance of safe dude horses we may need, and part of our pack string, we lease from other dude ranchers or buy them locally. We or our partners bring some of our horses across the mountains from over seventy-five miles distance.

Of probably more importance than suitable horses, although we take it as a matter of course, is securing the proper staff for the expeditions. As in the old cattle roundups, the "ramrod" of the outfit must have real "hands", not apprentices. Gathering at daylight of a hundred head of horses (called "Jingling" because of the bells on some horses) in the rugged mountain country, some down country five or six miles from camp, some as many miles in the opposite direction, scattered from "Hell to Breakfast", is no job for amateurs. Roping, bridling, saddling the dude's horses, getting the dudes mounted and away on the trail before eight a.m., is only a start. Saddling pack stock, tailing the pack strings, tearing down the complete outfit, packing up and pulling a string of five or six-pack horses over the "salty" trails, is no job for untried men or women. Mountain trained cowboys, ex-cowboys or other skilled horsemen are, of course, the answer. These boys with the experience and know-how are a must, and several of them come great distances each year to help with the rides. It is important to note that not all these wranglers are men, women are often a significant part of our crew, and do a considerable amount of the work as wranglers, cooks, and cook's helpers, and many of the tasks. This is doubly important, as so many of our paying guests are women as well.

Of equal importance to the packers and wranglers in the success of the trips are others—the cook, first mentioned because he becomes the best known and the center of all activities twice a day; activities shared alike whole heartedly, from the lowly dish washer to the President of the A.B.C. Railroad. Twice a day, morning and evening, his musical call of "Come and get it", echoes and re-echoes among the trees around camp, across the lake, and from the peaks in the background.

For many years we have been fortunate in having the services of one Monte Savage, world traveler, sometimes chef, in the finest hotels of the land, at others, by his preference, serving up, "Out of this world" grub at our trail ride camps in his beloved native mountains. The foregoing quote is that of lady trail rider's common comments, not mine. *Vie* natives eat it and say nothing, un-cinch our belts and come back for more, which Monte takes as his finest compliment.

The tent crew of four men, so called because they have a thousand other duties involved in tearing down, packing up, moving across a high timberline pass to another site, and setting up again a complete tent city of over fifty people each moving day.

This work is under the direction of our son Bob, who, back in his teens, first assumed this core responsibility.

Four super-athletic young men set up or tear down a big camp with all the speed and teamwork of a well-coordinated college football squad.

Bob, starting his first experience on pack trips at six months, riding on a big pillow in front of his mother, his older brother hanging on to her belt behind her saddle. She followed me wherever I had to go as a U. S. Forest Ranger in performance of my duties, learned horses and the mountains the hard way. Bob is now a first lieutenant in the Naval Reserve, engaged most of the year in active duty as a landing signal officer in the instruction and qualification of fighter pilots in carrier landing operations. He was aboard (and safely rescued!) the USS Block Island escort carrier in 1944 when it was torpedoed by Nazi U-boats in the Atlantic Ocean. He shuttles back and forth from his present duty station in Atlantic City to our home. One day in Navy uniform, four days later in old favorite Stetson, Levi's, and cowboy boots. "From an L.S.O. to dude wrangler in one easy lesson," as he describes the quick change.

Leaving Glenwood Springs last year on August 1, five of the boys drove our horse herd (remuda to Westerners) some forty-five miles up into the heart of Colorado's Elk Mountains, to our first campsite, near the old ghost town of Marble. All saddles, bridles, supplies and equipment, except the guest luggage, were trucked to the camp the same day. The cook, helper, and tent crew accompanied the trucks. During the day, the group set the camp up, ready for guests to arrive later.

The Trail Rider guests, the official representative of the Association, and the official doctor all arrive on trains throughout the day. A get-together meeting is arranged for the evening at our large resort hotel (typically, the historic Hotel Colorado). Besides the Trail Riders, there will be the supervisors of the White River National Forest, over which most of our trip is taken, and members of our local group who have not yet gone up to the initial camp.

After introductions have been completed and necessary talks made, Mrs. Thomson, or "Tommy" from now on, takes over the job of getting quickly and thoroughly acquainted with all. Fitting into this duty, or pleasure I should say, Tommy fits into the job as few others could. Twenty-five years' experience in handling mountain dudes, plus that from fifty to seventy-five percent of our Trail riders are women, helps a lot. Probably the greatest help of all, however, is her keen interest in people, all people, and her uncanny ability to meet thirty or forty strange faces at our get-together meeting, and before the end of the next day's ride, be calling each one by their given name.

I sometimes wonder if all dude ranchers, or others who serve as hosts to strangers in strange surroundings, realize fully the magic in using first names. Through Tommy's natural inclination to call everyone she knows by their first name, we have all seen the friendly, human reaction, and this practice is a must in our camps.

One of our guests, whom I will call Miss Theodora Uppercrust, age 60, President of a Women's College, appears on her Trail Ride application form, and at the get-together meeting, she looks every inch the part. The beautifully groomed grey hair, her gown of downright loveliness, the undeniable air of dignity and superiority to the common person, stands out to where you recognize her from the guest list before an introduction.

Next morning, she looks different, quite different. A brand new, broad-brimmed cowboy hat sits a bit uncomfortably atop the gorgeous hairdo, a red and white checkered shirt, blue denim Levi's, and shiny new high-heeled cowboy boots complete an ensemble of "East meets West" attire.

Her "air" is still there, however, and remains for probably part of the first day's ride.

At the first night campfire gathering, carried on, I might say, from day to day with no let-up, Tommy diligently endeavors to get her big family better and better acquainted. Next day, Theodora becomes "Teddy" to all.

Another guest, we will call the Honorable John J. Dignitary, U. S. Senator, becomes simply "Jack" or "Jack 22", the latter being the number painted on his saddle horse's hip, in case there are two Jacks in the party.

After hearing Tommy call out cheerfully before end of first day, "Teddy, if you don't quit letting your horse step on his bridle reins, I'll pull you off and spank your Levi's before all this crowd." and noting the pleasure and good fellowship in Teddy's eyes, you know she belongs.

Once with a guest list sent us from the Association office, was an accompanying letter announcing that Mr. So-and-so, the "great industrialist", and his wife would be a guest at the Trail Ride party. You could almost see the look of awe that must have been in the writer's eyes as they sent this profound news. The "great one" and his charming wife proved to be one of the best, most adored "John and Mary" perfect couples we have ever met.

Many people cannot grasp the difference between service paid for and delivered and that passed out in an honest, human desire to serve as a friend. Tommy's short, but salty talk before a campfire gathering one evening described adequately what I have in mind. "We are all out to crowd as much joy and pleasure in a short two weeks as we can. Our outfit wants to do all we can to make everything pleasant for you as your friends, but I'm afraid we're all darn poor servants."

I might also make comment, that a quarter of a century, of performing Trail Rides, private pack trips, or hunting camp trips, we have met but one person who failed to fit into this democratic scheme of things required to make a trip like this successful. More about that later.

The wranglers and the horses arrive at the starting campsite in the early evening and find the camp set up. Twenty-five canvas floored tepee tents, 8 feet by 8 feet in size, several larger sleeping tents, and a large assembly tent have been set in a semi-circle among the trees. In the middle of the circle, the cook tent, sometimes called the "cook shack," has been set up; this is a large 20 feet by 30 feet water-proofed tarpaulin stretched on a rope between two trees, the center approximately fifteen feet above the ground, and sloping to the front and rear to supporting poles and guy ropes. This gives a rather extensive area protected from the sun's rays and rain overhead but open all the way around. In the center of the shack is the chef's cooking fire, confined within a folding metal fireplace or stove designed for this purpose. To the rear of the shack is the cook's kitchen and storeroom. Toward the front side is a roll up table fifteen feet long and thirty inches wide, used as a serving table.

Just a few yards in front of the cook shack, in an empty space, the boys have skidded up an enormous pile of campfire wood, and in tepee shape is piled up a large campfire arrangement, all ready for lighting.

Our horse wranglers have the horses all in the corral, saddle horses each with a number painted on his left hip, starting from number one, up to the number that are needed, based on the number of guests. We similarly number pack horses, starting from the number of last saddle horse, and up to the total number used. All saddles, both riding and pack, are also marked with the corresponding number of the horse we have fitted them for, this latter mark being with an indelible pencil on surgeon's tape stuck on the saddle.

In the rear, at either end of the camp, are two small tepee tents, to enable the "necessary functions" marked with red paint, one for the "Bucks" and the other for the "Does". Now when I first marked these tents, they were properly designated, one as "Ladies", the other as "Gentlemen". With true cowboy spirit on one trip, before we arrived in camp, our wranglers had rudely erased my modest crayon work and replaced it with the glaring red paint they were using for the numbering of the horses.

At a little distance from the main camp, the horse corral and wrangler's tent are located, where horse's tack is stored. The corral is of double 3/8-inch ropes stretched around an area almost a quarter acre in size; the ropes held up by trees and stakes.

In the meantime, the prospective Trail Riders in town have arisen early in their hotel rooms, dressed in their outdoor clothes, packed their duffle bags and sleeping bags. They are allowed a total weight of fifty pounds for each person for their luggage, and this is ample. It is amazing what an array of necessities, "maybe come in handy", or "why did I lug that along" things one may pack within the weight limit.

Bell boys from the hotel rush the tremendous pile of duffle and sleeping bags to our waiting truck. Riders finally get the loose ends gathered, and by nine a.m. are all on the bus which will carry them to the first camp at Marble. After forty-five miles up the Roaring Fork and Crystal River valleys, the big bus arrives at the end of the road, and camp as previously described.

With a little stretching, introductions of the wranglers and cowboys in camp who have not yet met the Trail Riders—then Monty's lunch call soon rings out to the trail riders.

Behind the serving table, laden with steaming food, Monte, his helper, and our lunch girl (this year, Bob's new wife Jean) are ready to help the hungry over-fill their wants. In stacked piles at the right aid of the table as you approach, are stainless steel compartment food trays (a familiar sight to any ex-soldier or sailor of the late war), knives, forks, spoons, and cups. In regular cafeteria style, each one picks up his tray and tools and starts down the line. With a well prepared, efficient food serving for the group, all are taken care of in a matter of minutes.

Around the assembly campfire, the boys have drawn or skidded up a large circle of logs which serve as seats. With a log underneath, the tray resting on knees, one can eat a tremendous meal in satisfying comfort.

At the end of the meal, each one carries his tray and tools to the dish washers table, and his or her responsibility ends.

First task after lunch is the assignment of tents, each of which is numbered. The eight by eight-foot canvas tepee tents will hold the beds of two people, with a little space for duffle bag luggage.

Where guests have no friends or acquaintances within the group, and have not previously selected their tent pardners, they are paired up to the complete satisfaction of all and assigned the more permanent owners of "Tent 17" or as the number may be. Their luggage is taken to their tents, and soon all are ready and eager to try out their horses and saddles.

This horse assignment is a problem of combined tact, joy, sorrow, and real "hoss tradin". The most beautiful horse in the outfit may be a counterfeit of the worst kind. The poorest looking and altogether most unattractive horse may be, and generally is, or we would not have him along, the sure-footed, fastest walking, easiest riding, most intelligent horse we have to offer. One young lady of many college days, and much fewer horse hours, said in all earnestness, "I've never ridden much. Please give me a horse that hasn't been ridden much, and we can learn together." So, the wranglers do their best to match each person to the horse, which will be their riding partner for the coming two-week adventure.

Finally, all the guests are matched with their horses, stirrups fitted, and the group is off on a short afternoon ride to get acquainted with their horses and saddles. Tommy or Bob, with several wranglers, go along to guide the party, check cinches, and change stirrup lengths. All come back at five or six o'clock a little tired from their long day of train rides, bus, and initial horse trip.

Just at supper call, one wrangler lights up the prepared fire pile, and it instantly becomes a living thing, crackling and dancing flames casting their cheerful glow over the camp.

When all guests are seated around the big circle, I take stock of the group; I hark back over our ten years of providing Trail Ride experiences and can provide an average of what one might find in each group.

Thomson Trail Ride picture courtesy of Rebecca Thomson

The age spread would be from the tender age of eight, the daughter of one of our official doctors, on up a few years to the older in the group, who I, in fancy, will call Billy Williams. Seventy-nine summers had passed before Billy, then an attorney engaged in active practice in New York City.

He was a most competent and experienced happy Trail Rider, a never-ending source of good humor and fine company. There may be some family groups—Dad, Mother, and the two girls, or boys: lawyers, professors, businesspeople of various kinds, doctors, retired farmers, and many others on many walks of life. Gushing young women just out of college, teachers, secretaries, stenographers, some young, and some more mature, some well-to-do in worldly goods, others saving for an entire year to enjoy the two-week outing, — all good gals and boys. Doctors, over the years, have made up the larger group of professional men. On one trip we had eight! As I recall, it was on this trip, among our group was a famous psychiatrist, who in a campfire talk attempted to explain why tired and harassed people needed trips like these to bring them renewed life and vigor. Carried away by his subject, and possibly forgetting for the moment that there were many other doctors listening, he earnestly said, "I believe among all different classes of people, there are more doctors than any of any other group, who, in plain language, are a bit "different"—as a cowboy here might say, a little screwy." He stated that the different way of living experienced in camp life was what most of them needed. There were only a few suppressed titters at his statement—the other listening doctors only smiled.

Next evening at the campfire gathering, four strangely garbed men came somewhat late. Pants rolled up to the knee, a bright red necktie neatly tied around the calf of his leg, his coat and hat turned wrong side out, was the outfit of one. Others had their coats turned wrong side out, one with a tie hanging down his back, one with long red underwear tucked neatly in his cowboy boots, and a pair of chaps borrowed from one of the boys, covering the rest of his legs. This group, whom we immediately recognized as they came into the bright light of the fire, gravely marched over to the psychiatrist and their spokesman said, "Dr. XXXX, my colleagues and I request you to grant us an appointment on tomorrow's layover day. We would like very much to have a complete examination, and your opinion whether we are improving?" The odd group was composed of doctors, and after that, more than a few polite giggles followed, and a smile on the face of the famous psychiatrist.

On the first night out, there is often a welcoming talk by a Forest Service official, and brief talks by some of our group on safety precautions and camp procedure, and all retire early.

Most of the group use sleeping bags, regular manufactured bags of either down, wool, or kapok as the filler, depending on the warmth desired and the amount one wants to spend for them. They have a pocket on the underside for an air mattress, and with this outfit, plus the knowledge of the proper amount of air to put in them, one may have a mighty fine bed. At least they all think they are fine after a few days on the trail.

Arising at Monte's first call around six a.m., all are soon "washed up" with hot water from the cook's fire, combed, creamed, powdered, "lipped" and what have you for the girls—the men with maybe a tiny nip from duffle bag, a lick and a promise at their hair and wash basins. Some may break out a comb.

The welcome "come and get it" signal rings out. Behind the serving table, loaded down with hot steaming food, will probably be Monte, the lunch girl, Jean, and Tommy, as a combination public relations director and hostess.

At the fire making hotcakes, on large restaurant griddles are Monte's helper and "One Shot John B. Shutte", most of the time the postmaster of our fair city of Glenwood Springs, now, during his two-week annual vacation each year, official hot cake baker, photographer, and dude wrangler.

I stood just behind a gentle lady in one morning's line. She turned and said, "I've loved the smell of the pines and spruce, your lovely mountain flowers, the power of my horse as he carried me over the mountains, but none has the fragrance of this," and she waved her hand over the table. Feeling rather wolfish, I agreed.

Fruit or juices, hot oatmeal or cream of wheat, bacon or ham and eggs, hashed brown spuds, hot cakes or French toast and coffee all smell good in any man's country or camp.

Often a rather frail looking gal at the first breakfast will say, "One pancake only, please. I only eat a small piece of toast and a small glass of fruit juice at home." Monte and Shutte keep tab on this kind, and joyfully announce a week later that "Dorothy is now a ten-pancake girl".

Duffle bags and rolled sleeping bags assembled at the "pack pile" near the cook shack, all walk over to the horse corral. The boys, all of whom have eaten breakfast long before, have horses all saddled and tied to corral or nearby trees. With the help of crew members, all are mounted and off on the trail by eight a.m.

Tommy, Bob, or one of the Forest Rangers, over whose district we are traveling, leads the group up the trail. At the end of the long line of riders, our lunch girl (and my daughter-in-law), Jean, leads the pack horse or mule, which is carrying the fixings for our mid-day lunch.

Thomson Trail Ride picture, showing Tee Pee tents setup, courtesy of Rebecca Thomson

As the long line of riders climbs up away from camp, we are soon in the sub-alpine country. Scattered groves of the hardy, dark green spruce and fir are found on the slopes as we go higher, finally running out with the last dwarfed specimen at around 11,000 feet elevation. Between this "timberline" and the top of the pass over which we will cross lies the true alpine country. We may see negligible amounts of brush other than the low alpine willows in low wet places, the ground being carpeted with short brilliant, green grasses. Among the grasses are flowers of a thousand kinds—every color one ever knew is there. From the tiny alpine species, whose bloom is no larger than the head of a match, to the beautiful Columbine (Colorado's state flower) which grows at its best and in the most vivid coloring in the timber-line country.

To one side of the trail, we look up the steep and glacier marked slopes of towering peaks, still far above us, their tips clear cut in the thin air, or wrapped in a cape of rolling white clouds. Looking the other direction, we may see off in the far distance, and four or five thousand feet lower, the valley and road leading to civilization.

Although I have lived in the mountains for many years; served as a Forest Ranger over this area when a young man, the high country, has never lost its charm.

As we go along, Tommy shuttles back and forth along the line, kidding the men, greeting, or scolding the women, checking cinches, and "visiting". We made frequent stops to take pictures, movies, or stills, colored or black & white, as most everyone carries a camera. Schutte sets up his large camera at the most scenic locations, and "shoots the works"; this often being photos of the entire group, or subgroups, with always an impressive background.

Some guests start a flower collection. We carry a large plant press for this purpose. Others search for rock specimens or try their hand at panning gold from a likely looking streamlet.

As we climb higher and higher, far above the nearest timber, we run into scattered snow fields which we must skirt or go over their tops in some localities, sometimes this means the lead rider may need to bust down a short wall of snow which may remain from last winter's snowpack. This is not difficult if an experienced person takes the lead and rides the places where the snow is deepest. To a mountaineer, this is easy—the general appearance and ridged condition indicating the deeper parts. The first horse off the field will break through to the ground at about a three-foot depth, however, this horse will break out a good trail for others.

The crowd often stops for a snowball fight at these locations, it being considered somewhat of a novelty to have a snowball fight in August. These snow fields often answer the Trail Riders questions why we don't carry on the Snowmass-Maroon Bells Trail Rides all summer. We have, much to our sorrow in the past, tried to start the rides too early. The snow is just too deep until August 1, and horses cannot get over the passes. After August 31, the possibility and danger of encountering heavy fall snows is also too great.

Reaching the crest of the divide, or pass, each rider makes a brief stop to look over the country behind him, and that of the unfamiliar country ahead. Some of our passes are over 13,000 feet in elevation, often of knife-edge character, and with the chilly wind whistling through that light jacket, one is glad to move on down. Other passes may be in hog-back form, the day calm and warm. In these situations, a longer half-hour stop may be made by the entire group. They make efforts to pick out the route through the lofty peaks which the party has just traversed. Maybe a pass is identified over which the party crossed three days before. It may appear to be ten miles away, as the crow flies, but a checkup on the topographic map shows it to be forty, and many more by the winding trail we have been following.

Dropping off the pass a mile or so, a sheltered place at the edge of the timber, and where good water is available, we make the noon lunch stop. The place for lunch stop is the same each time we make this trip, selected because of not only shelter, wood and water, but for its scenic beauty, abundance of flowers and good feed for the horses.

The pack mule is quickly unloaded, campfire built, and two five-gallon cans for boiling tea and coffee water are placed upon the fire. At these high elevations, water boils quickly; We can brew tea or coffee in a few minutes. While this is going on, Tommy and the lunch girl lay out a long string of plywood trays, side by side, making a table of considerable size, and the lunch material is placed upon it. Bread—white, brown, and rye, butter, peanut butter, jam, honey, mayonnaise, mustard, lettuce, coleslaw, onions, pickles, tomatoes, and cheese; Lunch meat, salt, pepper, catsup, canned milk, sugar, fruit and cookies and various other good things our trail riders enjoy so much. Each guest goes along the table and plans the construction of their lunch from the materials at hand. While my plebeian taste has never got much beyond the simple ham sandwich with plenty of mustard, the sophisticated sandwich construction one sees here is something to remember. No two are just alike, except for the heavy construction and masonry-like buildup, layer by layer. Washed down with several big tin cups of tea or coffee, spiced with the loads of laughter, talk and good cheer, we can enjoy one of these picnic lunches "right smart".

After lunch, some take a little nap in the sun, others may walk out for a few pictures, collect flower specimen, or prospect for unusual rock or mineral to add to their collection. The horse wrangler keeps a weather eye on the horses, which have been turned loose with dragging reins to graze in the park. He must keep any of them from trying to roll, as this may break down the cantle of the saddle, not to mention any cameras or eyeglasses left in the saddlebags.

In the meantime, what of the boys back at camp we started from this morning? Following the departure of the Trail Ride guests, the camp becomes a scene of activity unequaled by anything except the moving day of a tent circus. Clock work, teamwork, or a united race against time might best describe it. A squad of four athletic speed boys hit a tent, jerk the scissors poles down, unlash the tie rope, jerk the corner tent pegs, and throw in rock, grab the four corners and fold for packing—all in less time than in the telling. Another cowboy shuttles back and forth on horseback, carrying tents before him to the pack assembly pile at the cook shack.

The cook and helper are packing in panniers, the utensils and food for the evening meal. The packers are tailing their horses in strings of five or six-pack horses, tearing down rope corral, their tent and beds and packing them on horses. Going then to the cook shack, which by this time has been torn down, they help the camp boys pack up about ten horses with tents, tools and equipment first needed in the erection of the next camp.

These boys start on their way, followed soon by the cook and helper with three horses packing the evening's supper essentials.

The packers left in camp, five or six with a large party, then pack two strings and start them on their way, always with at least two packers going out together in order that they may help one another in case of trouble. The last strings, with beds and duffels, get away from the camp ordinarily by ten a.m. or a little later. All go directly to the next camp without stopping, other than to "blow" their horses. They carry lunches in their pockets, a much less elaborate affair than the trail rider dudes enjoy.

To those who don't understand what is meant by "tailing" of the pack horses, each packhorse's lead rope is tied to the tail hair of the pack horse ahead, about three feet of rope being allowed between the halter ring and the half hitches on the tail of the horse ahead. The lead horse is, of course, led by rope from the halter to the packer's saddle horn.

In some localities, pack horses are driven ahead, but this is out of the question on our type of mountain trails. Good pack horses trained in this method seldom tighten their halter ropes, and we have not had a bad pack string accident since we started "dude punching" twenty-five years ago. Of course, we don't monkey around using broncs in this kind of perpendicular country, nor do we use anything but "rubber neck" packers, the latter being men who have learned to turn and watch their pack strings behind them.

During the lunch hour, or sometimes before, our Trail Riders have seen the camp or tent crew, Monte and helper go by, and have the comfortable and insured feeling that no matter what may happen to the balance of the pack string, supper and their shelter tents are before them.

With a pleasant lunch under their belts, the horses rested from the long morning climb, the afternoon ride passes quickly. New scenes at every turn of the trail keep up the photographer's interest. A detour and exploratory trip through the timber brings them into a small park utterly covered with tasty mountain mushrooms. All dismount and fill the two five-gallon coffee and tea boilers and all other vacant spaces in the lunch mule's panniers.

Often a wild raspberry patch or a park covered with the little wild strawberry is found, and all the "kids", young and old, get off and feast on them.

By this time, everyone in the outfit has become used to their saddle and fallen in love with his saddle mount. The considerable amount of "hoss tradin'" we expected has not materialized. Each has found so many good points that they completely over-balance the few prejudices they may have had at first.

Riding into our next camp in the late of the afternoon at from four to six o'clock, we find the big cook shack up and gently flapping in the breeze, all the sleeping tents up, the logs skidded in for the assembly fire and seats. Monte in his white linen and chefs cap, or check shirt, Levi's jeans, and Stetson hats, according to his moods or supply of clean "white" aprons, waves a cheery "Hi Jack or Hi Jill" as each one of the party rides into camp.

With luggage in their tents, all have cleaned up, put on their lighter, more comfortable camp shoes or moccasins, and maybe rested a bit before Monte's supper call.

Some, unashamed, fairly fly to the cook shack, others with slightly more decorum, but all faces alike cannot hide the anxious, hungry look of "high country" peoples. Roast beef, corned beef and cabbage, boiled ham, or steak, something equally appreciated by all as the meat feature. Vegetable or split pea soup, mashed potatoes, green beans, green stuff salad, and either of Monte's surprise desserts. One might wonder how juicy, big roasts, boiled hams, they could cook navy beans over a campfire in the brief hours since he arrived in camp and "got going". A roast is seared and baked a few minutes in our large Dutch ovens, nearly red hot and practically airtight. The cooks then move it directly into a six-gallon pressure cooker in which only a little water is placed. Set on the stove, the cooker quickly reaches a fifteen-pound pressure, at which pressure it is held for about an hour. Out comes one of the most delicious roasts you can imagine. Beans and a few other foods that can hardly be boiled enough in an open kettle to make them tender, without losing all flavor, in these high elevations, are pressure cooked in a little over an hour's time and come out as food fit for a king. The sun sets early in the valleys of this high country, and air blowing over snowfields and glaciers becomes cool, sometimes chilly, after sunset. The huge blaze from the camp assembly fire, however, keeps the area nearby very comfortable, and all enjoy its warmth while eating.

Some few modest souls, during the first meals in camp, go behind the nearest tent and loosen up their belts a few holes, "for more comfort", they later tell Tommy. After a few days it is good form to stand up before the eyes of the world and uncinch a few holes of the belt, not altogether for comfort, but with the honest and frankly stated desire to make room for chef Monte Savage's dessert of the evening.

Following supper, (never called dinner in the mountains) riders take a little rest in their tents, go fishing, hiking, picture taking, or help clear up the dishes, or watch the horse wranglers replace lost or loose horseshoes.

As darkness creeps over our little tent town, all drift into the assembly fire and select their favorite log seat. Our Association representative selected for his ability to meet people and make friends with all, often serves as a song leader. Songs from popular music "hits" to grand opera, old and new, all sound beautiful as their echoes and re-echoes come back from the mountain walls and mix with the next lines of the song. Monte, no longer a cook, becomes a Burrill Ives with his western ballads. George Shaw, the wrangler during daylight, brings up his guitar, joins Betty with her mandolin. Stories, experiences, and jokes by clever tellers of tales, and we do have many "clever people" throughout the land, all go into making the evenings go fast. We hit the sleeping bags early, and how good they feel. Assuming that the following day is a lay-over day for the party, we have four such days on the Snowmass-Maroon trip, this to provide some rest for the camp crew and relaxation for all.

The lay-over camp sites, which had been previously selected, are on a good fishing stream or on the shore of a mountain lake where fishing is good. At the Snowmass Lake lay-over camp, everyone sleeps a little late this morning. Breakfast drags along for an hour, at least. Monte becomes nervous as he rigs his fish pole, and to one of the late coming horse "jinglers" who has just finished his breakfast, "Jake, go over and tell Slitz and Blatz to come and get it, or I'll go over and drag them out." "Slitz" and "Blatz" are not their real names, however, they were so inclined to always bubble over with the joy of life, and being natives of that famous Milwaukee area, their common names were soon lost to the more descriptive titles. I cocked my ear for Jake's message to the girls, though there was no need. In a bawling command that crossed the lake and came back in double echo, "Youse gals had better skin on your breeches and git up to breakfast or Monte will kick your pants and take your cigarettes away." This dire threat, common to the cowboy vernacular, with a few slight changes, had the desired effect. In a few minutes, up tripped "Slitz" and "Blatz", pink pajamas slipping down below the rolled-up Levi's. "We came just as soon as we could, Monte. We know you're such a dear boy you wouldn't care." Monte, a perfect setup for that kind of talk, melts into his usual good humor, grabs his fish pole and tramps off to the lake for some wilderness fishing.

One group of six or seven hardy souls leave camp intending to climb the mighty Snowmass Mountain, extending up well over 14,000 feet into the clouds. Led by Mel Griffith, a noted Colorado mountain climber, who sometimes is a member of our outfit, the group goes around the lake shore and starts the climb from the opposite side of the lake. Their course leading them up over talus slides, cliffs, and snow fields nearly the entire distance within sight of camp. We "camp stool climbers" sit at one of the large log table and bench combinations which the Forest Service provides at well-used camps, and with our field glasses, "sweat it out" in considerable ease until the climbers reach the top.

Others do a string of laundry, colorful as the flowers growing under the line, and a source of considerable embarrassment to our cowboys who ride by, head bowed, and their free hand, held over their eyes! Only peeking a "little". Some of the more daring don their bathing suits and plunge into the icy waters of the lake. Fed by glacial streams, the water of Snowmass Lake seems colder than ice. Our official doctor (one always accompanies the party), often an M.D. of national renown, calls out in dismay, "I advise against it".

The shock of that water is too great. "Don't do it." Falls upon deaf ears. "Doc", as he is affectionately known, almost has a "hissy" (what that is I have never learned) as he notes the pleasant disregard of his advice.

He finally realizes that he is not dealing with patients, nurses, or obedient interns, and sits on the shore with the same expression as I imagine he uses, when, informing the anxiously awaiting relatives near the bedside of the sick one, "There is no hope".

To rub sand into the wound, one well past middle-aged gentleman, (whom I afterwards learned took his plunge into the ocean every day of the winter) calls out in mock alarm, "Oh Doc, I'm about to have cramps, what shall I do, better come out and get me." Just to be "safe and sure", as the saying goes, I mosey up to the horse corral and get a saddled horse and lariat, and ride back down to the shore of the lake. The boys always accuse me of wanting to get a closer view of the mermaids—perish, the thought—anyway, that is all that has ever happened, despite Doc's and my misgivings. Some in camp just eat, sleep, fish, loaf, or assist my son Bob with the barbeque.

The day before, he has secured a fine fat lamb from one of the nearby sheep camps. From early morn until supper time, he, his wife Jean, and volunteer helpers have been turning, basting, basting some more, and turning the lamb over the hot coals of a barbeque pit. The aroma arising from this job penetrates the air throughout the camp, extends out over the lake to the fishermen, thence up the walls of Snowmass, and greets the returning mountaineers, still a thousand feet above us.

The fishermen have been coming in at various times for a snack and coffee and keep building up our camp supply of beautiful native and rainbow trout. A little woman named "Madge", who had never fished for trout, decided she would try it out. Her only tackle was a short, coiled piece of heavy line, a too large bait hook, and some bacon strips from the kitchen for bait. Tommy helped her find and cut a willow pole, and she took off toward the far side of the lake. After several hours and most of the experts back in camp, Tommy walked around the lake to see what luck her friend was having. Her path led through a heavy patch of timber on the shoreline, close to camp, and as she entered the timber, she met a young fellow she knew from our hometown of Glenwood Springs. He greeted her, "Mrs. Thomson, I've got a dozen fine trout more than the law allows. I started to go down through your camp when I saw a couple of Forest Rangers over there. Can I give the trout to you?" Her reply was, of course, the natural one of a mother with over fifty hungry mouths to feed. Holding the willow strung trout in front of her, and away from sight of camp, she reached Madge and learned that her luck as a fisherwoman had failed completely. "Here's a string of fish. Don't you ever dare to tell that you did not catch them," said Tommy, who then returned to camp. Soon Madge came tramping into camp, lugging the big string of rainbows.

It would be nice if I could say that Madge stuck to Tommy's instructions and never divulged the truth. The barrage of questioning by everyone in camp, the questioning too exacting, too many she could not answer—in a burst of half sobbing and half laughing, maybe more of the first, she said, "I just can't lie like you men do about your fish or fishing, Tommy gave them to me."

With everyone finally back in camp safe and sound, washed and dolled up, we are ready for our lay-over day supper. The sun is dipping over the crest of Snowmass Mountain, fairly riding, or resting on the snowbanks, which gives it its name. The odd purple tinge of this hour creeps into the shadow of the gulches. As the daytime winds die down, and the lake becomes a fairy mirror. Snowmass Mountain, upside down, rests against the opposite shore, and the mountain tip lies just under our feet on the still lake water. Peace is with us, and all is well.

Bob and Jean come marching through camp from the barbeque pit, the brown sizzling lamb securely lashed by wire on and around the long pole which has served as a rotating spit, carried on their shoulders.

Monte, his helper, and Schutte are finishing cooking the last frying pans of the fried, golden-brown trout, the other foods steaming on the warming part of the stove.

Monte strips off the wire holding the lamb to the spit, and under his trained and flying knives, the lamb is cut into sizeable, eating pieces within a few minutes.

Tonight, the crowd is not sitting at the assembly fire awaiting the supper call. Nearby everyone is crowding around the front of the cook shack, watching the carving, gazing intently, like a bunch of hungry kids at a candy store window. No, they are not the kids, the whiners, or yearlings of our party, they are the regular run-of-the-mill of from fifteen to sixty-eight winters, all unashamed in their eagerness to chow down tonight.

When we are all seated around the campfire, our trays filled to top heavy proportions, Doc breaks in with what he considers timely advice, in his best professional manner, "I know you are all hungry, but your stomachs will hold only so much. I don't want any acute indigestion cases on my hands." Like all unpaid advice, his warning fails to gain the attention given his opinions by the President and Brass Hats of the armed forces during the late war. All fall-to on the dark browned, medium, or rare succulent mutton, trout, and other good things of the day, and stop only at the last buckle hole in their belt, leaving only space for Monte's surprise dessert which he keeps as a dark secret until serving time. On this evening it is blueberry dumplings. Many express regrets at their failure to have left enough room, some even cautiously releasing the belt buckle entirely and trusting to luck and the waist band buttons. Poor Doc's good advice, completely ignored, resulted in no ill effects, or hardly any. Doc, an hour or more after supper, quietly strolls up to where the cook is clearing up the kitchen. "Monte, do you have a little baking soda? I believe I ate a bit too much."

When checking the first rough draft of this article, it appeared that I had given undue space to the subject of food, and that some would wonder how we could pack sufficient food to supply fifty or sixty people on a two-week trip. We don't—on four different occasions we are close enough to roads extending up into the wilderness that the packers go out with a string of horses and pack in fresh supplies that have been pre-positioned to the end of the road, by one of our stay-behind employees that has a pickup truck. I started to say we packed in fresh meat, bread, green garden stuff and other perishables, harking back to our first expedition. We then packed enough staple foods to last throughout the trip, securing only the perishable goods from the outside. This resulted in an unwarranted number of packhorses, or too heavy loading at the start of the trip, so we have learned how to do so more efficiently.

With Monte's knowledge of foods and quantities required, Tommy's knowledge of what tastes best in camp, Bob's analysis of the packing end, and my rather extended experience in methods used by logging, mining, forest service and army camps, we went into a huddle and solved the food problem.

Before the trip starts, menus as a guide, non-perishable foods are packed beforehand in stout packing cartons of a suitable size for packing in the panniers. We tied these up with binder twine, their contents plainly marked with crayons. This permits sending out with the supply truck only the food required for each period. This supply, with the addition of perishable goods, will last to the last meal of a particular period, no longer. After the last heavy meal before a fresh supply comes in, Monte's food panniers are as bare as "Old Mother Hubbard's Cupboard."

Streamlining of other equipment is likewise the rule. Our cooking and serving tables, stoves, harness, tool kits, toilet seats and other camp equipment have been designed with strength, lightness, and folding up compactness a must.

After our first lay-over day, we travel for several days, always in a new country. Conditions are about the same, each day crossing over a pass high above the timber line, following the winding trail for mile after mile.

A word about these trails—left to nature, they would soon fade into nothingness, with hardly a scar to mark their location. The Forest Ranger on whose district the trail is located inspects them frequently during the summer and keeps a small crew of skilled trail men busy in maintenance work.

Most of these forest rangers of the mountains are great credit to their Uncle Sam employer. Competently resourceful, and intelligently handling a mighty big job, we and the guests appreciate their ever-ready help in "smoothing the rough edges" as we ride along.

Camping one evening on the shore of Crater Lake during a previous trip a few years back, the site being selected because of the unusual beauty of its location, immediately at the base of the Maroon Bells, the tents were setup in the rich green grass close to the lake. During the night, it rained, and from the grass arose untold thousands of flying insects, probably a close relative to the willow fly. The insects were harmless but invaded all the tents. No one slept too well, however, with one exception: the guests arose happy and cheerful as usual. They crowded around the cook's fire and the tremendous assembly fire nearby. Our cowboys had been up since four a.m.; the wranglers ranging far and wide to gather the horses, the camp boys rustling wood and preparing for a move that day, rain, or shine. All were soaked to the hide, tired already, and with the dreary prospect of moving a wet camp. They were taking a few minutes off to have some hot coffee. Suddenly from one tent a man appeared, waving his arms, and crying, "The bogs (bugs), the bogs, the bogs." This gentleman was of foreign birth, a wealthy refugee, and of comparatively short residence. He came to the fire in an icy rage. "The bogs, the bogs, they stop my sleep." Then followed a tirade against the weather, the country, and more particularly "the darn fool tent crew" who had placed his tent in with the horrible "bogs".

Picture of Crater Lake taken by Daniel Parliman in 2003, no "Bogs" encountered that day. Daniel Parliman digital image.

I did not hear this conversation, being over at the cook shack having my coffee with Monte, then I noticed the dead silence at the assembly fire—moments before a bedlam of laughing and kidding among the boys and the guests—I sensed nothing wrong. Glancing that way, I saw my son, Bob, then in his late teens, talking to the man and tapping him on the chest with his stiffened finger. Bob's normally cheerful face was like a thundercloud, his usually laughing eyes fairly screaming with anger. Standing nearby, their coffee cups in the grass at their feet, arms hanging low from half crouching shoulders (I learned to know and recognize this pose of a primitive man about to start a battle in the lumber woods many years before) were four of five outraged young men. Dropping my coffee, I jumped from the serving table and rushed toward Bob. "What's the trouble?" "Dad, I just told this gentleman we would throw him in the lake if he opened his mouth again." Getting both sides of the story, I requested the gentleman to go with me to my tent. There, in the most diplomatic way possible, hampered somewhat by an undiplomatic desire to howl with laughter, I explained our democratic way of life in America, more particularly in the West, and "for keeps" on wilderness Trail Rides. I gave him the choice of being sent out with one of the boys to the nearest town, or an apology to the boys for his unwarranted abuse. With some gentle combing of his ruffled feathers, a salving of his outraged dignity, he finally confessed he had acted unwisely. Further talk brought forth a gulping sob that "outrageous" was the proper word, and that he thought the boys were truly wonderful men. We returned to camp and shook hands all around. He placed an order for four quarts of Canadian Club on the commissary order book by the now cheerful man. "Maybe it will make the boys happy on the next rainy day, and maybe they will give a little to me too," he stated with candor.

Several evenings later at campfire talk, the "Gentleman of the Lake", as some ladies dubbed him, made a talk that pleased me greatly, and I believe the entire group as well. In broken English, but easy to understand, he commented on the wonders of America, his joy at leaving Europe and becoming one of our magnificent land, and last, his extreme pleasure in being a member of our fine trail ride. Quoting as near as I can recall of the part of his talk, I liked best: "In Europe I always like the climb of the mountains, I climb, climb all the time. In Europe, I must hire two or three "mans" to go with me. We tie ourselves together with ropes like mules or goats. We plan for two days and climb only one. It is much bothersome. In America your hardy young "mans" just dig a trail and ride your horses up on top of the highest peak. When your young "mans" have no time to dig a trail, they just ride their horses up on top of peak anyway, and holler down to the rest of us, "Come on up, what to hell you fraid of?" I believe I clapped louder than anyone. I felt like he was talking about our outfit's particular boys. That's the kind they are.

The term "boys" might be a little misleading to those not familiar with the way many of us Westerners handle the "King's English". One of our boys on a trip several years ago was Si Bailey, cowboy, packer, horseman from the Lower White River country. One of the most active, competent, hard working all around "Hands" in Colorado. His seventy-two years were carried so lightly that one of our doctors asked him "how come" he was such an active, strong man at his age. "Shucks", said Si, "You oughta see my pappy. He was comin' with me as a hand on this roundup, but a bronco he was breaking pawed him down and broke his arm just before the ride." Of course, Si was doing a little "dude baiting", however, his "pappy" was a very pert young man of the nineties at that time.

The evening of the last lay-over day is normally selected as "stunt night". The riders by this time have become very much, one big family, hardened to the rigors of camp life, happy and self-sufficient in their mode of life as it is here. This latter was so clearly demonstrated on one of our first Trail Rides, I have not forgotten it. At one of our grub supply contacts with the outside, and after we had been out for ten days, I brought to camp a copy of that day's issue of the Denver Post, the leading newspaper of the Rocky Mountain region. After glancing through it, I carefully placed it on a big rock within the assembly circle, thinking to myself of what a beating the poor lone newspaper would take when all the riders got into camp. When this happened, one man, a stockbroker, walked over and turned the pages to the stock market report, glanced at one item, smiled a bit, then carefully folded the paper and placed it back on the rock.

No one else seemed to notice it and after a while, being a little peeved at no over interest in the paper which I thought would be so much appreciated, and which I had so carefully carried in my shirt front to avoid crumpling, I called it to the attention of the whole party. I received only one reply. An elderly gentleman whom I would bet had not missed reading his paper each day for years, who dryly remarked, "We don t live out there anymore, Rich". Next morning as I rode over the camp area after all riders had left, a custom to pick up cameras hanging on tree limbs, gloves on a rock, loose toilet articles, and other items, there laid my Denver Post on the rock, its pages as smooth and unread as though just off the press. "I got no time to read a paper, there's other things to do.", so I put it away, to use it on that night's fire.

Stunt night brings out an array of talent, unexpected by the most optimistic of those arranging it. Dramatic theatrical skits, comedy, poetry built up to fit the trip and party members, a square dance with the old calls of fifty years back, and in the old descriptive wording of the ranch news reporter. "All had a good time."

Meeting the bus far up in the mountains above Aspen, once a big mining town and now the ski center of the Rocky Mountain country, the guests bid goodbye to their horses. Many an old cow pony receives a hearty kiss on his nose, and a tight hug of his neck, and a tidbit that has been carried along that day for the parting.

The bus ride back down to Glenwood Springs, with a brief detour through Aspen to look over the lower terminal for the longest ski lift in the world at that time, two and three-fourths miles, is accomplished in a few hours' time.

Meeting at Glenwood's large resort hotel, the Hotel Colorado, later that evening, we again greet a crowd of strangers. Fresh haircuts and shaves, gorgeous hairdos, and city clothes all do their part in making a wondrous change. As we become accustomed to the dazzling lights, we recognize our riding companions. The beauty parlor operator has done her best, but the little skinned place on Sally's chin (She forgot to dodge a low hanging tree limb) still shows a bit and identifies her- despite the evening gown she now wears. Dave has kept his two weeks crop of whiskers but has had them trimmed up. In his dinner jacket, he looks exactly like one of those foreign dignitaries we see in the movies as they attend some big time something or other. Dave looks like he knew this perfectly and accepts the kidding and compliments with equal pleasure.

At the banquet, attended by all Trail Riders, all members of the Thomson HH outfit, and a few members of the Forest Service, many toasts of goodwill are spoken, and washed down with the liquid beverage of choice. With the old American standby of Auld Lang Syne, the trail ride is regretfully brought to an ending.

The tearful goodbyes at the Denver & Rio Grande depot later in the evening, as trains depart for east or west, complete the picture of the summer. However, in some years, several months after our trips, we receive a large envelope, postmarked from some small town back east—Albany, New Haven, or other. Tommy opens it as we sit at our breakfast table, flips out an inside envelope and lets forth with a squeal of surprise and delight. "What do you know? An announcement of Betty B. and Hank's marriage. Who would have thought that?" Duke Lyons, our year around horse wrangler, speaks unsurprised, "No surprise to me, I saw Hank holding her hand at our last night campfire." I have no comment. Many years of observing and remembering have taught me that a great many things can happen in the mountains—and so often does just that.

THE END.

THE LAST THOMSON HUNTING CAMP
BY DANIEL PARLIMAN

This is a true story. I have changed a few of the names for various reasons. Partly because I may not totally remember all the names (it was fifty years ago!), or even know if all the people mentioned are still alive and kicking. To the best of my recollection, it describes true people and events, and reflects the Colorado stories I heard growing up, as well as my experiences after moving to Colorado in August 1972, as a 16-year-old. That fall, I spent almost two months at the Flattops Ft. Defiance hunting camp, managed by my great uncle, Robert W. Thomson. I turned 17 while at that camp.

First, I would like to summarize the main characters and events involved and I will acquaint you with others who you will get to know as this story proceeds. Some of these people you may have met in the previous content of this book, but I will attempt not to be overly repetitive.

R.W. Thomson, my great uncle (often called "Uncle Bob"), married my grandmother's younger sister Jean, on January 1, 1946. He had been born in 1920 in Telluride, in Western Colorado, but lived in Glenwood Springs, Colorado most of his early life. As a teenager, Bob started assisting his father, Rich Roy Thomson, and his mother Pearl (called "Tommy"), and older brother R. James (Jim), in their extensive outfitting and hunting camp operation. Bob left Colorado College (now Colorado State University) in 1942 as so many of the "Greatest Generation" did after the bombing at Pearl Harbor, to join the US Navy. After training, he was on the one US aircraft carrier to be sunk by the Nazis within the European theater of the war. That sinking happened on May 29th, 1944, just off the west coast of Africa. After the war, he continued with both the Navy in a Reserve officer capacity (carrier training and anti-submarine warfare training), and by carefully using his annual 30-day Navy leave; he continued with his family's hunting guide and trail ride outfitting business as much as possible. He did have other scattered occupations during the 1950s such as prospecting for silver and uranium, and as a "fish spotter" pilot off the coast of New Jersey, in which he would locate schools of fish, then radio its location to the fishing fleet. In 1949, he began guiding elk and deer hunters in western Colorado every fall uninterrupted, with his last hunting camp, taking place in 1972.

Around just before 1960, as he ended his Naval reserve duties as a Lt. Commander, and he and my Aunt Jean moved back to her hometown of Woodbine, New Jersey; they founded a combination restaurant and sporting goods business, called the "Colorado Café". I practically grew up at the Café, and was close to Aunt Jean and Uncle Bob, and besides the business, they were our next-door neighbors during the sixties. At the end of the Sixties, they moved back to Glenwood Springs, where they purchased a larger fine dining restaurant called "The Red Steer Restaurant", and they continued with their hunting camp business.

I first heard the stories about Colorado and the hunting camps, stories about Grandpa's "DeCinque Hole" buck, the 66 switchbacks of the Defiance Trail, and stories about "Nunny's Cave Spring" while growing up as a very young student in the early 1960s. Probably my two biggest impressions in those days were the Colorado stories and the exciting space launches taking place at Cape Canaveral in Florida. The Colorado stories were heightened in importance when my DeCinque Grandparents took me out to Colorado about the time I started kindergarten. I did not get to go to hunting camp itself that year. I did get to the Ft. Defiance trailhead in Glenwood Canyon and was able to swim in the famous Glenwood Springs Hot Springs Pool. We stayed at Uncle Bob's mother's house and met "Tommy" for the first time. In later years, my grandparents would take my other siblings on their annual trip out west, so we all got a turn.

Most of my maternal family lived in Woodbine, New Jersey, in those days. For those of us who grew up as the 1950s and 60s which later became known as the "baby boomer" generation, this aspect of living with family surrounding us was typical then. Although not so much typical now as I look back, fifty years later. My parents in those years (who later separated and divorced by the time I was in sixth grade) had a small early 1950s cinder block 3 bedroom, 1 bath house. They now call them subdivisions. Directly across the street from us lived my great Aunt Gloria (Grandmother's youngest sister) and her spouse, Uncle Carl (WWII Vet). My Great Grandfather George (Hrynko Stasyshyn) Stanle also lived with them as a recent widower. Right next door to us, also in a cinderblock house, lived my great aunt, Jean, with her husband R.W. (Bob) Thomson, previously mentioned. Still on the same block, but on the opposite corner of the block, lived yet another great aunt, Helen, and her husband, V.I., also a WWII vet. My Aunt Mary lived on an adjacent block, just 1 block away. My maternal grandparents Henry & Estelle DeCinque, his son Henry DeCinque Jr (Uncle Nunny) with wife Carol (and my great grandmother Rosa DeCinque lived with Carol and Nunny) were next door to each other about 6 blocks away from us. Another one of my grandmother's sisters, Sophie, lived with her WWII vet husband, Sonny, about 4 blocks away from us. Sonny was in the US Army Air Corps, was shot down over Holland in WWII, and spent more than a year in Stalag 17 as a guest of the Luftwaffe. To round out the roll call of family in Woodbine, my grandmother's brother Michael lived with his spouse Rose about 8 blocks away, Michael was also a WWII Vet, as were the two other brothers Frank and James who lived near to in Woodbine as well. All of my paternal relatives of my dad lived at least 20 miles away in Cumberland County, in Millville and Vineland, New Jersey. Back then, I thought they lived so very far away, but now seems so much closer.

I guess it would be a real understatement to say that I grew up with a fair amount of my maternal family, living within walking distance, or at most, a quick bike ride away. With having so much family, so close, was probably why day care centers existed very little in those days. Our schools were also close by, and never had to ride a bus to school, until the 9th grade.

Around 1960, was when my Uncle Bob and Aunt Jean opened up the Colorado Café and Sportsmen's Center in Woodbine. It was mostly a sandwich focused restaurant, with counter stools, booths, and some larger tables, and a small sporting goods store, inside the restaurant which had firearms, ammo, etc. Sporting goods were located to the left as you entered the restaurant. In the back were a couple of pool tables, some pinball machines, a jukebox, and in the very back was a medium-sized room, occasionally used for banquets, along with some work and storage rooms. The Colorado Cafe menu used names that surrounded my uncle's life, for example, a (freshly made) cheeseburger with lettuce, tomato, and fresh cut fries was a "Colorado Burger" and a grilled steak sandwich was a "Buck Hunter" and with melted cheese a "Trail Rider."

The "juke box" was your normal Seeburg juke box, at that time playing the great hits of the Sixties, except my uncle, added a couple "special tunes". I would play them occasionally. One song was a bull elk "bugling" a high-pitched call, the other was a screaming mountain lion, a high-pitched, snarling sound. I don't recall the servers, or customers enjoyed hearing those tunes.

At the very front entrance, my uncle used one side corner to display the rifles, shotguns, ammo, and related hunting gear that he typically sold. He mostly marketed to those people looking for rifles and scopes for planned hunting trips out west, including many of the local area hunters who were his guided customers for elk and deer trips to Colorado, although some ammo was sold to local NJ hunters as well, as hunting was popular around that area too. On several of the back walls next to the "Sportsmen Center", were displayed various deer and elk trophy mounts, bear rugs, and mountain lion rugs, etc. Several of these were sourced from Thomson's Colorado hunts from Uncle Bob, or my Grandfather Henry DeCinque Sr, or his son Henry Jr (Uncle Nunny). My Aunt Jean also displayed many of her antiques around the restaurant as well.

One marketing technique that my uncle Bob used at the Colorado Café to great effect, was during the winter he would typically have one or more "wild game nights" where some of the elk and deer meat harvested the previous October in Colorado was deliciously prepared (with homemade cowboy gravy) by my Aunt Jean. This was served to the hunters, or prospective hunters, and also, they would show them their 8mm or 16mm color, narrated Colorado hunting camp movies showing their previous successful hunts. I have no doubt this helped in acquiring new hunters for the following year. I still have two of these movies (converted to DVD & now digital) and they still have that effect on me.

Daniel Parliman Family picture of Colorado Cafe, Woodbine NJ

Many other of our extended family members did also work at the Colorado Café at various times, including my mother, who was a server there. Often I would do various jobs even as a small child, like sweep the steps outside, and shovel snow (although snow was rare most years). Mostly, I would be paid with my aunt's homemade soups. Later I started to help take care of the guns using a silicone cloth, to get rid of finger smudges from people handling them. Often, especially after second grade, I would go to the "Café" after school on many days, as my mother generally worked days. As I got older, I would tag along with my uncle, especially after he sold a rifle and scope, and watched as he would take it to the target range, and sight-in the scope for the customer.

But the thing I enjoyed the most at the Café were all the marvelous stories that the adults would discuss. Stories about the hunting camps, and various individual stories about various people and events. My grandfather, Henry DeCinque, was often a daily customer at the Cafe. When I was not in school, I would often look for his work truck in the Café's parking lot, knowing he would invite me to lunch, and share his stories, or he and Uncle Bob would tell their stories, and I would just listen. I learned how Uncle Bob had started at an early age helping his parents with Colorado trail rides or the hunting camp outfitting business for so many years; also, how his dad Rich Thomson was one of the first Forest Rangers in the White River National Forest and had worked in various other National forests throughout the west. Prior to the forest service work, Rich had worked on various ranches and was well known as a rodeo cowboy, especially related to saddle bronc rodeo competitions.

His mother, Pearl Thomson (everyone called her "Tommy"), was heavily involved in the family outfitting business and was well known as a "cowgirl" and for her horse-riding expertise. She was very important to leading and managing the summer trail rides and their horse rental business they did for many years in western Colorado.

Pearl Ellis Thomson c.1920, Family Picture

Bob had assisted his mother in the trail rides after Rich had passed away in 1950, when he could get away from his duties in the US Navy. Since the late 1940s, Bob had taken over as the primary Thomson person in running the hunting camp part of the business. My grandfather Henry DeCinque Sr. was a paying hunter of Bob's starting in 1949, not missing a year all the way until the early 1970s. They were also brothers-in-law, and very close friends. Besides their common interest in Colorado hunting, they were also both very qualified pilots, so aviation was a common topic of conversation at the Cafe too. One story they used to tell concerned a trip they both made to pre-Castro Cuba in the late 1950s, that included partying and drinking rum, were activities of note; although they did get into some deep-sea fishing as well. Flying back to Key West in their small plane, there was a problem with their "paperwork", which required some urgent phone calls to arrange clearance to return to the US.

Henry DeCinque Sr c1966 Family photo. Daniel Parliman digital image

Many other hunters from South Jersey made the October journey to western Colorado during those years, not just from the Cape May County, but from neighboring Cumberland and Atlantic Counties.

Several were from Millville, and often these local hunters would stop by the Cafe to tell their stories as well. In their Avalanche Canyon hunting area in Colorado, Thomson named one place "Millville Sidehill" to honor these Millville NJ hunters. In later years, there were several of his hunters and associates from New Jersey who ended moving out to Colorado, some who live there to this day.

Every fall, usually in mid to late September, Bob (and usually Jean), would pack up their station wagon, sometimes also a U-Haul trailer, and head west, to prepare the camps for his hunters. As mentioned previously, a good portion of them were from South Jersey, although there were many from other states. The key ones I recall were Pennsylvania, Illinois, California, Wisconsin, and Texas. For many of the years Bob ran his hunting camps, he was fortunate that he could store most of the camp equipment at Horse Haven, his mother's house in Glenwood Springs. Especially for the years in the Navy or when living in Woodbine, this allowed him to store the bulkier things like horse saddles and blankets, tents, stoves, etc., rather than haul that equipment cross country twice a year. When Rich and Pearl were younger, they typically owned a fair number of trail horses. They would lease additional horses based on the number needed for their summer trail rides and autumn hunting camps. After the trail rides ended in the early fifties, Bob switched to leasing most of the horses needed for each fall's hunting camps, since they were needed for two months or fewer. Since they typically leased horses from the same suppliers, many of the horses were familiar to the crew (and even the returning hunters), as they would often lease many of the same horses every year. I recall that for many years my grandfather was assigned a horse he liked every year, named "King".

Typically, I hung out at the Colorado Café several times a week, listening to either Uncle Bob or Grandpa tell their stories, or other family members such as Henry Jr. (Uncle Nunny) would be there, sometimes other hunters and friends.

I also went often to my grandfather's house, or next door at Uncle Nunny's. It was an interesting time. Uncle Nunny also hunted deer in

New Jersey during both archery and shotgun seasons. Sometimes right on his kitchen table he would cut up a deer, while his wife, Aunt Carol, would fry some of the loin, and packaging the rest for storing in the freezer. What my aged great grandmother, an immigrant from Italy, who lived there at the time, thought of that, one can only wonder.

In the back room of the house, he had his "trapping" room, a place where he would skin the muskrats, racoons, fox, etc. Throughout grade school, Nunny would sometimes invite me on trapline "runs" with him, as his own children were still very young at that point. Sometimes I would wait in the car, while he checked his muskrat traps on the Jersey tidal meadows (I was too small and did not have hip boots yet). In later years, when I was a very young teenager, I ran my own trapline for a brief period, and trapped with a friend, within walking distance of Woodbine. I recall in those days there was still a bounty on fox, and we would send the ears to the county. I assume the bounty was because there used to be many poultry farms in Cape May County.

Back in those days of the early to mid-sixties, every fall, we were aware that Uncle Bob, and Grandpa (and often others) were off hunting in Colorado. Aunt Jean and other spouses would also sometimes stay in Glenwood Springs with friends (often to stay with "Tommy"). But usually by early November, the hunters would return to Woodbine, usually loaded with elk meat in boxes of dry ice to keep it frozen. Normally, we would have a few family gatherings, featuring fried elk meat, cowboy (country) gravy, and mashed potatoes. I can still taste it now, many decades later.

In the off-season, there would be one or more "planning sessions" at the Colorado Café whereby Uncle Bob and typically my Grandfather Henry Sr, Uncle Nunny, and others would get together to plan out the details of next year's hunt. Where are we going to hunt next year? Will it be in the Avalanche Creek area of the Maroon Bells Wilderness, or the Flattops of the White River National Forest? If so, where on the Flattops? South Grizzly or the Ft. Defiance? I would try to be there to hear their discussions if I could. Uncle Bob would always put a binder together for each year, for example in the winter of 1960/61 they planned "Operation Avalanche 1961" which was going to be the first year of hunting the upper Avalanche Creek region, part of the Maroon Bells Wilderness Area. In that year, only a few people planned to go so they could learn about that hunting country. Just my Uncle Bob, Grandfather, and Uncle Nunny, and a few hunting camp staff, and a couple of short-term guests. In the years following 1961, Thomson would have larger camps with something like 25-30 paid hunters. But that first year in Avalanche, the group was kept small so the country could be learned and properly guided in the following years.

In these "planning sessions" they would plan the details of what gear and equipment were essential and required. This planning was to try to "minimize" pack loads, keeping in mind that their packhorses would have to carry all that gear about 10 miles deep into the wilderness, away from any road or resupply point. Cooking utensils, food, clothes, sleeping bags, how many pairs of "long johns"? How many oats for the horses? What permits were required from the Forest service? Plan things like how many candy bars, apples, bars of soap, and how much prune juice to avoid constipation. Would a -10 degrees below zero eider down sleeping bag work, or do we really need one that will work to -20 degrees below? Of course, back then, it had to be from Eddie Bauer. Once the number of hunters was known, Bob could calculate the number of horses to be leased, amount of horse feed, hobbles, and bells for the horses, etc. How many staff to hire? Some of these were Colorado or Kansas ranch hands, or college students, some were rodeo cowboys, experienced trail cooks, other cooks were cordon bleu chefs, others worked in various other restaurants. Even some were Colorado Café workers from the Woodbine area.

Back wall of Colorado Café, with mounted Deer most of these were taken at Ft. Defiance hunting camp, near one is Henry's, DeCinque "Hole" buck. Daniel Parliman Family Picture

My Uncle Bob was very particular concerning the rules that his hunters had to agree to, to take part in his camps. For example, he was adamant about handling firearms safely, and no alcohol while hunting (afterwards in the tent is ok though). He especially had rules about using a significant caliber firearm. He did not want to wound an animal needlessly, so he published rules beforehand that hunters had to agree to, or else they could stay home. For example, a 30-30 or 30-06 were OK for mule deer hunting, but he did not allow his paid hunters to use them for elk hunting. With large game like elk, 7mm, .300 Winchester or higher were typically required. For those of you who remember the great debate in those days between Outdoor Life's Jack O'Connor who promoted the .270 and shot placement, versus Guns & Ammo's Elmer Keith's large caliber & velocity usage for big game, R.W. Thomson was squarely a supporter of his good friend, Elmer Keith's position. Jack's .270 did not make the cut of allowed firearms for elk hunting in the Thomson camps.

One other aspect of Thomson's hunting camps I would mention is that he tried to make the hunting camp experience be interesting to his paid hunters, as well as being a safe environment. He would strive to have decent cooks available, so the hunters enjoyed their meals, and plan to have a doctor in camp, just in case one was needed. I remember him saying that he would not actually pay the doctor, just provide him with a free hunt, including food. He mentioned it was easy to find a doctor, as there were many who enjoyed hunting, and they liked free stuff.

To facilitate the paid hunter's learning of the country they hunted, Bob would name significant points of geography around the camp, with common sense, memorable names like Lion Spring, Bloody Texas Gulch, Big Buck Ridge, or Wapiti Basin. He used real names where they existed from Forest Service map names, examples: Wagon Gulch, Hell Roaring Creek, and the Ute Indian trail. He did this for several of his different hunting camp areas, both on the Flattops and the Avalanche Creek hunting areas. He ordered topographical maps (or purchased aerial photos) and hand write the names and give each hunter a map to keep with him. There was no Google Earth available in those days. If there was, I am sure he would have used it. When he told someone to stay put at Lion Spring, or rendezvous at 3 Bear Park, he would expect that person to be there. Below is an example of one of the Avalanche Creek hunting maps, found in the papers I inherited after his and my Aunt Jean's passing. They often changed these maps from year to year, as unknown places were named. Please also notice rules designed to keep hunters safe, or what to do when lost, are listed on the map. This map is missing place names I am familiar with, so it may be a map, from earlier in the 60s. If I locate any more detailed maps or related photos in the future (I encourage others who have any to please share also!), I will attempt to provide them at my publisher's website:

https://www.GrizzlyCreekPublishing.com

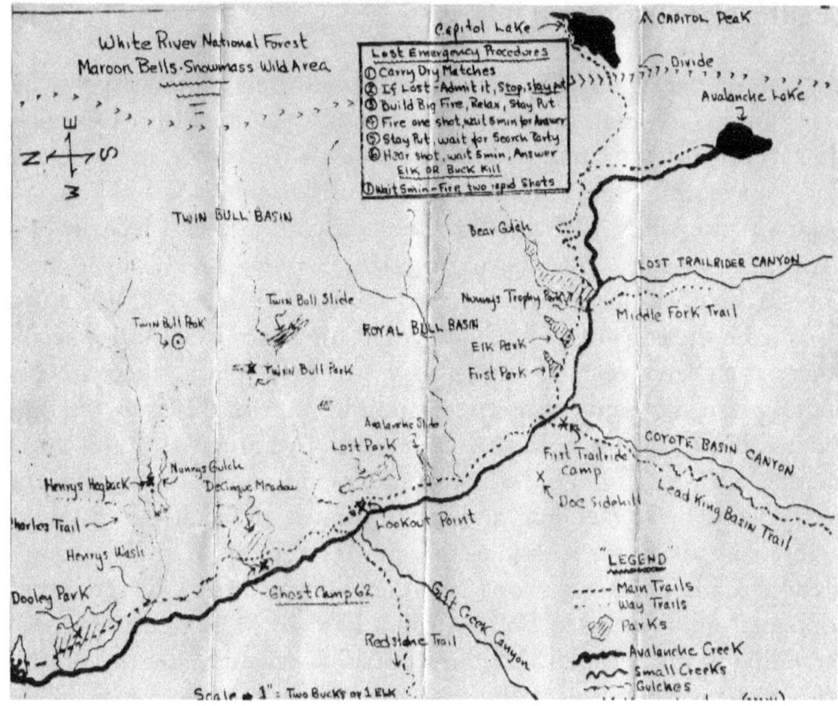

Map by Robert W. Thomson. Daniel Parliman digital image, c. early 1960s

He also would sometimes hire a couple of his hands, not so much for the work they could do, but also regarding their "entertainment value" to his paying customer, his hunters. One I can recall was a rodeo clown (and guide and rancher), George Shaw, who could sing cowboy songs very well and was very entertaining. George was also mentioned as providing similar services in Rich Thomson's description of the Wilderness Trail Rides. Then there were the Buttram brothers, Matt and Jim. In the 1960s, Jim was well into his mid-70s, with Matt, the baby brother, being 13 years younger, enjoyed telling stories about each other. They were originally from Missouri-Arkansas border area, with supposedly some way back kin connection to the James family (yes, those James boys, Frank and Jesse). More on them later.

During those days at the Colorado Café, here are just a few of the stories about the hunting camps and Colorado that I recall:

The Buck at DeCinque Hole

My grandfather, Henry DeCinque Sr., would often tell the story of his first hunt in Colorado in Thomson's Flattops Camp at Fort Defiance. He called it his "DeCinque Hole" buck. This took place in 1949, at a place not more than a 20-minute walk from camp, near a sinkhole at a point overlooking the Colorado River canyon, known as Glenwood Canyon. It was also not too far from the Grizzly Creek Canyon area. The sinkhole was just on the edge of the canyon overlook, just a few yards from the edge of an Aspen covered forest above it. A very scenic point, as in later years I was to visit the exact place when archery hunting near that same area. The "sinkhole" part of this story was just a naturally occurring hole that developed over time as water from melting snow ate through the limestone, creating a hole that was maybe 5o feet wide by 5o feet long, and maybe almost 35 feet in depth. There were many of these sinkholes within several miles of Thomson's Flattop Camp. Another one in the Defiance region reportedly contained multiple bison bones from a herd of Mountain bison, that according to my uncle, died out in a horrific blizzard in the 1870s. This effectively was the last of the mountain bison (a sub-species of the plains buffalo) in that part of Colorado, and this happened at least 10 years before any significant number of white settlers settled in those parts. I had wanted to find that buffalo sinkhole, but years later, when I had the opportunity, it just never worked out that I was in that part of the country, with enough time to look for it. I suspect those bison bones are there till this very day.

Grandpa Henry in 1949 was in his first year of Colorado hunting, in Thomson's camp on the Flattops, also called Ft. Defiance. He was not a very experienced western hunter at that point, nor in New Jersey, although over the next 20 years that would change. I have no doubt Thomson and his cowboys/guides called him a "Jersey Dude" in 1949, just as my brother Dale and I were called "Jersey Dudes" when we were in that same hunting camp in 1972. So, early in deer season, Grandpa was placed by the edge of the sinkhole, at the edge of the aspen grove, in the very early morning. He waited for a while, straining his eyes, looking for any movement among the backdrop of the canyon rim and golden aspen trees, as the morning light slowly increased. Suddenly he noticed a very large mule deer buck, standing still, less than 100 feet away! Minutes went by. I am sure grandpa was thinking, how did that buck get there without him noticing the movement? Was it there all along?

As he later told it, as time went by, the buck still standing still as a rock, he became sure that the boys were playing a trick on him; thinking they had maybe brought a painted plywood buck with real antlers, and they were just waiting for him to blast away at it. A trick Henry would play on two Woodbine friends decades later near his aircraft hangar. But still the deer did not move, but eventually something caused him to think it was a real buck. Maybe he could see the buck exhaling on the brisk October morning. Anyway, he shot the buck with his .308 Winchester, and they later assisted him in hanging up his cleaned kill on the camp meat pole. They skinned out the head, and later packed it down to Dawson's Taxidermy, and for most of the 1960s, it hung on the east wall of the Colorado Café in Woodbine. It had a plaque in which Thomson told the brief story (see the picture below of original plaque).

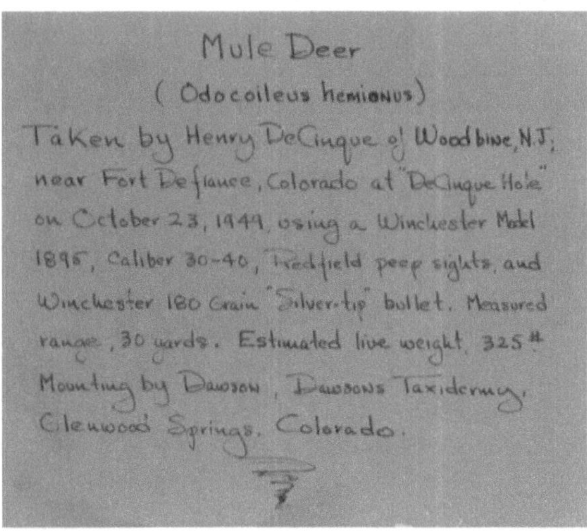

Original Plaque used for DeCinque "Hole" buck, first used at the Colorado Cafe, then moved to the Red Steer Restaurant approx. 1969. Daniel Parliman digital image.

Later in life, I would experience how mule deer could absolutely freeze for many minutes when they sensed danger, in that same country, but about a mile southwest of DeCinque Hole; I was approaching what we called "The Slick Hill Trail", and I saw a decent buck very close, 30 feet away stand totally frozen and who continued to stand stock still, as I pulled up the reins and stood motionless watching him. In this case, I did not shoot as my deer tag had already been filled earlier, and I recall that it was elk season only at that point as well. But that buck stayed still for a good ten minutes, even though I was so close.

Arizona Ray

Besides the camp help that my uncle Bob Thomson would hire, mostly from Colorado or Kansas, he sometimes would hire people from Woodbine or the surrounding area. This was specifically to work in his hunting camps, and sometimes they would help travel to Colorado together, either in the same vehicle or a small caravan. Some of these were people who worked as cooks or other jobs at the Colorado Café, others were local people who had outdoorsmen skills, etc. One of these was an interesting guy they called Arizona Ray, who I believe was from Belleplain, NJ., and I think he worked at one of the Ft. Defiance camps in the late 1950s. He supposedly had a deep voice, and was a very down to earth, direct person, but also would be of the type to believe whatever someone told him. Supposedly (this was retold to me in the early 70s, when I was in camp) some cowboys started telling him, prior to the hunters arriving, in a low-key manner, that in a couple of weeks there was a "big dance" planned nearby in a place called "Sagebrush Saddle". There would be all kinds of girls, music, a big party, etc. This "Sagebrush Saddle" was an actual place on the hunting camp map, but not very close by, and some place a new person from Jersey, who would mainly work around camp, would normally not get to without being taken there.

So, while all the boys were setting up camp, each night one of them would add a bit more to the story to Ray about the upcoming dance.

Finally, when the big day approached, sure enough Ray started spiffing up his appearance, using the wash basins regular, combing his hair, shaving (which is rarely done by anyone at camp), putting on his best shirt, etc. I guess when he started asking directions on how to get to Sagebrush Saddle; the boys let him down gently that there indeed was no dance being held there. But they had their fun, and from the way I heard it, Ray was very well liked by all.

There was one other add-on to the "Ray" story that Thomson mentioned about Ray that probably tested Thomson's patience just a little. On the drive out to Colorado that year, Bob assigned Ray to help him drive out to Colorado. Now, in those years in the late 1950s (or perhaps 1960), the roads were not the 4 lane Interstate Highways that exist now. It was mostly US Highway 6 & 24 back then, 1 lane each way, mostly. Often, they would drive all night, although occasionally they would pull over and sleep sometimes, maybe get a motel room, but rarely.

Bob started driving when they left the Colorado Café in Woodbine, NJ, and drove until well after dark, somewhere deep into Pennsylvania. As Bob told it after he switched so that Ray was driving, and he was deep in sleep, in the middle of the night, he was jolted awake, as Ray had pulled off to the side of the road, abruptly stopping the car.

Bob asked him, "What's the matter?"

Ray replied, in his deep voice, "Sorry Bob, I just can't drive over a bridge, any bridge." I am sure Uncle Bob probably at least thought some expletives, if not outright voicing them, as he was not shy and was for sure thinking why I am I just learning this now with dozens if not hundreds of bridges to cross in this 1800-mile journey? But as they adjusted, Bob drove his station wagon over probably what was the Susquehanna River bridge, and they continued their westward journey. Looking back on it now, Bob was probably glad to get to Kansas and those hundreds of miles of prairie, with relatively few bridges. Knowing Uncle Bob, he probably did not mind too much, as when I was around him, he preferred to drive, anyway. Although it was sometimes scary driving with him, as he would often close his eyes briefly when driving long distance at night, and if my Aunt Jean would mention it to him, he would say, that he only dozed on the "straight stretches."

Even though Ray worked just that one year at hunting camp in 1959 or 60, he was still remembered in stories told around hunting camp supper, over 10 years later, in 1972 at the camp I attended.

PleaseDontKeelNobodyBasin

One day during the sixties, I was looking at a map on one of the side walls of the Colorado Cafe, a map of the Avalanche Creek hunting area, that Thomson began using as his go-to hunting area, starting in 1961. As mentioned previously, it was his idea that when hunting with a group of people, that he would "personalize" the place names, based on events that happened, and related to the geography. So, as they hunted Avalanche for most of the sixties, place names such as "Millville Sidehill" where some hunters from Millville, NJ had some early success in that area, and it was added. Likewise, my grandfather, Henry DeCinque Sr., shot a large Mule Deer buck in a very large grassy park surrounded by Aspen trees in 1961, which was forever named "DeCinque Meadow."

When I was probably 11 or 12 years old, I was looking at that map, and saw a place name that said: "PleaseDontKeelNobodyBasin". I had to ask about it. Thomson told me the story. He said that a couple years before he had gone out to Colorado in a preparatory visit as he often did in the summer, to examine his equipment such as saddles, blankets, harnesses etc., and to get fixed anything that needed fixing, buy replacements when needed, i.e., to get ready for camp. Along with that, he would sometimes take a ride to his intended camp area, scout for elk, and verify that any "cached" equipment survived the winter and survived any marauding and curious black bear incursions. Porcupines can cause damage too, as they sometimes chew tents for the "salt" they may have. Normally, the type of equipment cached would be very bulky items such as metal stoves, large canvas kitchen tents, sometimes smaller tents too.

For this "check" visit, to their Avalanche Creek camp location, he was able to engage his friend, and sometimes hunting camp employee, George Shaw, to go with him. George, as mentioned before, was a very experienced cowboy, and very professional trail rider entertainer. He sometimes also leased hunting camp horses to Bob and others. He was also a very well-known rodeo clown. I remember he visited the Colorado Café one time, and I thought that his rendition of "Who shot a hole in my Sombrero" was way better than the old Rex Allen recorded version.

Back to the story, so Bob and George ride up to their Avalanche Creek cache. I assume they had one or two packhorses, since it was at least a two-day trip, in and out, especially if doing some side scout trips. They get up to the camp area, and then go into the dark timber to their "hidden" cache, and when they get to it, they see at once that it has been messed with, and not by a bear. Several things were just gone. It is hard to remember now, 55 years later, but recall he said at least one tent and stove were missing.

Now both men were experienced game trackers, but given the meadow contained recent evidence of sheep grazing, including their distinctive droppings, George and Uncle Bob followed the tracks until they finally dropped into a remote "basin" where they came across many hundreds of sheep, and of course the shepherd and his camp. Bob related to me in his story. He was not sure if the man was of Basque or Mexican origin, but certainly spoke Spanish. This was clear as Bob and George drew their six-guns, as they could plainly see their missing camp gear nearby in plain sight. Uncle Bob was typically packing iron, and this was not the first citizen's arrest he had made.

As Bob relayed this to me, the shepherd immediately and repeatedly said, "Senor, Please Don't Keel Nobody, Please Don't Keel Nobody, Please Senhor, PleaseDontKeelNobody," repeating this over and over.

Well, they gathered up their gear, re-cached it, and took the culprit down the mountain. I can't remember if they also called the sheriff, but they did call the owner of the sheep and released the "culprit" to his boss, after getting assurances that their camp "cache" would not be bothered anymore. It never was bothered after that, except by four footed critters. And the Thomson hunting camp revised map was forever named: "PleaseDontKeelNobodyBasin".

Hog-Lawed

This is a short one. I have previously mentioned the Buttram brothers who worked many of the Thomson camps, both in Avalanche Canyon, and on the Flattops during the 1960s to the early 1970s. Through the years, Jim Buttram would often mention how he had to leave Arkansas in his early youth, for general hell raising and various other indiscretions, some named and some not. Not only would he tell these stories in hunting camps, but even after the last Thomson hunting camp in 1972, he would come over to the Red Steer occasionally to visit, sometimes to shoe the few horses that we still had in the Red Steer pasture for a few years later.

In one of those visits, Jim was in his early 90s at that point, he was invited to lunch with several of my family members (and friends from NJ). He again told the story how he had to get out of Arkansas because of the warrants out against him for his various hell raising, including riding into a church, and discharging his pistol. Another house guest who happened to be a superior court judge from New Jersey asked him, "Jim, did you ever go back to face the charges in Arkansas to clear your name?"

Jim replied, "Nah, never did. I HOG-LAWED them instead!" The judge, his curiosity piqued, said, "I know a bit about the law, but what is HOG-LAWING?"

Jim Buttram replied, "that is when you leave a place for so damn long, they forget all about you." I think at that point he had been away from Arkansas at least 60 years.

1972 – Dan and Dale Move to Colorado

In midsummer of 1972, I was sixteen, my younger brother Dale was fifteen, and we were offered an opportunity to move to Glenwood

Springs with my grandmother's younger sister Jean, "Aunt Jean" and her spouse Robert W. Thomson, "Uncle Bob". Both had been our next-door neighbors back in Woodbine, New Jersey, for about ten years. But about three years before, Bob had been disenchanted about continuing to live in New Jersey. He was unhappy about the fact that his long-range rifle shooting range, at the Woodbine airport, had become unavailable to be used for that purpose anymore. I remember the day when he said to me "I am moving back to Western Colorado", and they did move back.

In the time since he made that declaration, he and Aunt Jean had sold out his interests in the Colorado Café in Woodbine (sold to two of Jean's other sisters and spouses), packed up their belongings, and moved back to Glenwood Springs, Colorado. There, he leased an existing restaurant called the Red Steer, located just off the exit in West Glenwood Springs. Of course, he continued his elk and deer guiding business each October. The restaurant was probably 250 yards as the crow flies from the Colorado River. In the ensuing years, I would make that walk underneath the Interstate-70 underpass frequently, to fly fish for (mostly) rainbow trout, particularly in the evenings, until I went away to college a few years later.

Red Steer Restaurant Sign   Family Photo, Daniel Parliman digital image

Bartender is author Daniel Parliman c1977, person in blue shirt is Don Hogan, was cook at 1972 Ft. Defiance Camp. Family Photo, Daniel Parliman digital image.

Salad Bar area of Red Steer; Elk is from 1972 Defiance camp by R. Thomson approx. 600 yards 338-378KT, bison is from Aug 1972 from South Dakota as described in article. Family Photo, Daniel Parliman digital image

My brother and I arrived in Colorado in early August 1972. We knew, of course, about the upcoming Thomson hunting camp in the fall. After we moved in with them, and both of us began working at the restaurant (washing dishes, bussing tables, etc.) which was open six days a week, closed Mondays. The restaurant opened at 5pm, so we had some off time during days, and I recall Bob and Jean taking us on a couple of fishing trips and picnics soon after our arrival, on Mondays. One of those was on the Roaring Fork River, one of the better trout fisheries in the country, also fished and had a picnic on the Crystal River, just below Marble, Colorado, where Uncle Bob had relatives near there.

Not too many weeks after our arrival, Bob arranged a trip to South Dakota with an acquaintance of his who owned a ranch east of Rapid City. For this trip, he rented a U-Haul trailer to be pulled by his station wagon. The aim of this trip was to shoot a Buffalo (Bison) and bring back the meat to be served in the Red Steer Restaurant for special buffalo dinners, etc. I believe my uncle paid the rancher for the value of this animal, my belief at the time was that the rancher needed to reduce his herd. I did not think then, or now, that this was a real "hunt", just a way for the rancher to reduce his herd. Uncle Bob prepared us for the taking of the buffalo. He designated me as the first shooter, my brother Dale as 2nd shooter, if needed, and himself as backup. For this purpose, he lent me his Champlin-Haskins rifle, chambered in 338-378 KT, my brother had another rifle chambered for .300 H&H, and Uncle Bob had his .378 Weatherby Magnum. As mentioned, before it was not a real hunt, the rancher drove us to his pasture where the herd was located, and the three of us were in the back of his pickup. The rancher showed us which bison to shoot, and when it was safe to do so (no other animals behind it), I aimed just at the short neck, and squeezed the trigger, and the bison dropped in its tracks. The rancher went after a front-end loader. Then we proceeded to field dress and skin the animal, as Bob wanted to get the quartered bison back to his meat processor and the head/hide to Dawson's Taxidermy of New Castle, Colorado. The three of us headed back to Glenwood. I never knew if Bob had been planning to do this all along or did this because my brother and I had recently joined them in Colorado, and still to this day do not know the answer to that question.

R.W. (Bob) Thomson, Dale Parliman, Dan Parliman Aug 1972.   Family Photo, Daniel Parliman digital image.

The trip to South Dakota, I am sure, took place over a Monday restaurant off day, most likely a Sunday night through a Tuesday morning trip. I do not recall Aunt Jean being on that trip, so she probably stayed back managing the restaurant.

On another Monday, I remember a day trip to the upper Colorado River area near Kremmling, Colorado, where we had a picnic outing, and caught some decent sized trout. Other Mondays that fall, we had a picnic up the Crystal River, below Marble, and I recall one in Glenwood Canyon, at the mouth of Grizzly Creek. On these outings, typically Bob and Jean would bring already prepared salad fixings, and some steaks we could grill. Even then I liked my steak at least medium-well to well done, and I am sure I endured at least a dirty look from Thomson, if not one of his lectures about only a "Jersey Dude", would cook a steak that well done. Guilty, and still that way.

The other major event I recall, prior to going up to the Ft. Defiance hunting camp, was a trip to extreme northwest Colorado, around Maybell Colorado, north of Craig, and east of the Dinosaur National Monument area, (and near to the Wyoming and Utah borders). This was in early September, as best I can recall.

Uncle Bob had sent into the Colorado Division of Wildlife, getting several antelope permits, and we spent one Monday up there trying to find antelope to stop running long enough to get a shot at long range. Finally, between my brother and myself, we were lucky enough to bag a couple of Antelope and bring the meat back to Glenwood. I recall that trip being a very LONG day trip and was disappointed that antelope meat did not taste anywhere as good as elk or bison, or at least that is my memory.

As September advanced, Bob increased his preparations for the upcoming planned hunting camp, planning how many tents, horses, saddles, packsaddles, horse hobbles, bells, and, of course, food supplies. Some (most) of this was already owned by Thomson and/or family, however some saddles and pack saddles etc. were provided when the horses leased for the upcoming camp, were delivered on the morning we first went up the trail to the Ft. Defiance camp in a group.

1972 – The Flattops – Ft. Defiance Hunting Camp

For this camp, my recollection is that the horses were provided to Thomson by his friend, Thurman "Fum" McGraw. Fum was then a rancher from northern Colorado, previously a standout football player for Colorado College (later Colorado State University), and former all-pro football player for the Detroit Lions. He also is a member of the College Football Hall of Fame, in Atlanta.

Behind the Red Steer restaurant, Thomson had several acres of pasture, and at the time of the camp, owned just three horses, a big palomino called "Yellow", a dark blue horse called "Blue", and a younger horse Bob had recently purchased, who he named for a legendary Ute chief, "Colorow". For most of the rest of the three dozen horses needed for this year's camp, Thomson leased them from Fum, and as I recall, they were trucked directly to the closest point the semi-truck could unload, nearest the trailhead.

The trailhead we planned to use was about ¾ of a mile west of the Shoshone Hydroelectric Dam on the Colorado River. It was on US Highway 6&24 in 1972, although nowadays the more than $500 million dollar stretch of Interstate 70 that goes thru Glenwood Canyon has replaced those roads. Back in those days, it was a two-lane, busy highway, at that point just North of the Colorado River. South of the river, the Denver & Rio Grande Railroad (and Amtrack) has a track with many daily trains traveling through the canyon, then and now, a busy railroad. The area where the trailhead started had no room for anything but a couple of parked cars. The plan was for the horse trailer to upload about a good half mile west of there, where a larger parking area existed, which allowed the horse truck to back up and drop its ramp to offload the horses. This also provided space so smaller trucks could offload the tack: blankets, saddles, pack saddles, camp equipment, and initial foodstuffs.

A little more about this trail we planned to use. Around 1879-1880 there was a small, attempted settlement established on the northern rim of Glenwood Canyon, called Ft. Defiance, about the same time as the Ute native inhabitants were being chased from the area. The original founders of Ft. Defiance were former Leadville area prospectors looking for new rich finds. Not too long after the founding of the mining camp of Ft. Defiance, many of the founders became disenchanted with it (probably from the deep winter snow, and ore that was a lot more lead than silver), and moved to what is now called Glenwood Springs, about 6-7 miles to the west, and down the Canyon. There are reports that a couple of people hung on at the original Ft. Defiance location, perhaps intermittently, as long as until the early 1900s. Anyway, after its discovery, a trail was snaked down the walls of the canyon, with sixty-six switchbacks. As far as I recall, it was never an official White River Forest trail that was "officially" maintained, as many other trails are to this day. The Thomson family, however, used the trail starting from about the 1930s when they had hunting camps at the former "Ft. Defiance" site for many of those years. Based on various research I have done, Ft. Defiance was used by Bob Thomson in the years 1949-1960, although in a few of those years, they used another site several miles to the west, in the upper Grizzly Creek canyon area. During the 1961–1969-time frame, the Avalanche Creek area within the Maroon Bells Wilderness was the primary hunting camp area used, although, in one of those years, the Grizzly Creek site was the camp selected. I know that from my grandparents hunting movies that show my sister at a young age, at the Grizzly Creek location.

Once Bob and Jean Thomson moved back to Colorado, he had returned to using both the Grizzly Creek and Ft. Defiance areas, and for 1972, Ft. Defiance was the planned hunting camp area. Most of the original miner's cabins had long since deteriorated by the time of the 1972 camp, with only a very few remnants of one or two partial cabins left, just a few logs.

It is now fifty years since we went up that trail that first time; I do not know the exact day, suspect it was around September 20th, 1972, but the one thing I can clearly remember is that it was a miserable rainy day as we began the journey. I quickly put on my slicker as the rain started. My slicker was one of those bright, blaze-orange slickers often used for hunters. If memory serves, on that first trip up to Defiance, there were at least ten, maybe as many as fifteen in the party, plus packhorses. Several of the people were part of Thomson's setup crew (Ron and Zella Brink for sure), to be supplemented as more of Uncle Bob's paid staff would join in the weeks ahead, with the main hunting season taking place during October until the first week of November or thereabouts. Of course, also in the party were my Uncle Bob, and Aunt Jean, my brother Dale and myself, plus a couple of people from the Red Steer Restaurant. Some people in that first group just stayed a few days.

That day fifty years ago is still memorable, as we assembled in the unloading area, with all the gear spread around, the wranglers busily leading horses with halter ropes, putting on horse blankets, riding or packing saddles, etc. Truthfully, I was scared; and ashamed to say I had never ridden a horse before that day (other than a pony ride). I had the gear, boots, and a cowboy hat and recall watching others, asking questions, etc., trying to learn quickly.

The assembly area was about a half mile from where the trailhead began. The scariest part of the journey for me was that I was handed a lead rope with two pack horses (one tied to the tail of the one I led), and we all began moving up the highway from the assembly area. My goal was to try and stay on the shoulder of the road, as cars were going by. Trying to avoid the pack horses invariably straying onto the highway area and not drop that lead rope or let the pack horses get hit by a car!

Finally, we got to the trailhead and started up the first of the sixty-six switchbacks. As we did, I noticed a photographer taking pictures. At that time, I did not know the back story about it, but later learned the photographer had met my uncle at the Red Steer bar the night before. When My Uncle explained he was taking a group of people on horseback to set up a hunting camp the next day, the photographer asked to take some pictures of the event. Fast forward several months later, my family received an autographed copy of a book, by National Geographic (award-winning) Photographer, Bruce Dale, called "American Mountain People". If you look at page 150-151 there is a two-page picture, with my Aunt Jean leading, followed by my Uncle Bob and most of the rest of us trailing behind obscured by the buck brush except one wrangler down the trail, to the very right. The photographer really timed the shot perfectly, because in the upper right background, a Denver & Rio Grande locomotive is heading east on the other side of Glenwood Canyon. The caption in the book reads "Pack train of elk hunters edges up a chaparral-covered hillside as a freight train passes through Colorado's Glenwood Canyon."

That photo was taken on probably the third switchback of the trail and, unfortunately, the only one I have of that entire trip. I contacted the photographer, Bruce Dale, and he graciously gave permission to use it in this book, but because of it being split on two pages of the book, I had to split it into two separate photos as shown in two photos below:

Jean and Bob Thomson, leading pack train into Ft. Defiance September 1972, Jean was riding their horse "Blue", Bob was riding his horse "Colorow", named for Ute Indian leader. Photo by Bruce Dale, used by permission.

Rest of group on trail, mostly in brush. Train in Background. Photo by Bruce Dale, used by permission.

Leading the two pack horses was much less stressful once we were on the trail. You had to make sure you did not follow the horse ahead of you too closely, watch out for branches scratching you or the horse, etc. The lower part of the trail had a lot of thick vegetation. I don't recall if my uncle had any of his staff prepare the trail prior to our first trip, but it was possible he did. As we continued up the trail, traversing the switchbacks, it started opening, and the view of the Glenwood Canyon became ever more impressive. We saw or heard several trains go through the canyon. As we climbed up about ¾ of the way, the trail seemed to be mostly out of the heavy buckbrush found below, much more open. One could see the entire party more clearly, and many miles of the beautiful Glenwood Canyon scenery.

As we reached the last several switchbacks, I became apprehensive, as the upcoming sections of the trail had a much greater steepness, with a potential drop-off more dangerous if one should fall. This last part of the trail came to be known to us as "the cliff trail". I don't recall if I voiced my concern, but I heard my uncle above us, reassuring us that, "remember, these horses want to live, just as much as you do, and they have four feet!" I made sure the lead rope for my two packhorses was in my left (outer) hand, and my feet were prepared to exit the stirrups, just in case my horse was not inclined to love life as much as I.

Ahead of me, I noticed my uncle, riding his horse Colorow, get to a steep part of the cliff trail that included a rock "stair-step", and his horse initially refused to climb that "stair-step". He raised his voice and goaded the horse, and said, "YOU CONFEDERATE SON-OF-A-BITCH!" And with a little more goading, then his horse climbed that step! I don't recall my brother's horse, or my horse, or the packhorses I was leading having a similar issue on that step, but I was sure glad a few minutes later when we had reached the top of the switchback trail. Then the trail flattened and became wider, to what was called "Wagon Gulch", with a trail two abreast could ride, and we were now among the very green mixed forest typical of the Flattops, with Engelman Spruce, and Aspen trees, and intermittent thick grass, about waist high. I could breathe again.

What was to be our Defiance base camp area was located a few minutes ride, further up Wagon Gulch. We soon got to a place with an opening towards our left. After less than a hundred yards through grass and interspersed aspen trees was a small water tank, my assumption being that the sheepherders who sometimes used this area in mid-summer had dug it years before, but that is just my guess. Above the tank was a miniature springlet of water, that had, as its source, a spring, with a small but sufficient steady stream of fresh water pouring out of a pipe, the excess of the spring flowed into the tank. We were at Defiance Camp.

Picture of the Defiance Camp area, taken in May 1973 backpacking trip, Daniel Parliman digital photo.

If one were to orient how things were located at camp, slightly above the water tank, and to the left of the spring, was the main area where the big 16x20 Kitchen tent was to be erected. Most of the sleeping tents were to be scattered above this, when erected. Most of the crew, including my brother and myself used the small teepee canvas tents, which require the corners to be staked, and then several long poles (aspen or spruce trees cut for that purpose), were raised up, with the rope at the top of the tent, tied to the triangular poles.

Lots of activity happened at once. The experienced wranglers took over, guided by Thomson. Pack horse panniers were taken off pack horses. They took some of the riding horse saddles off. A temporary rope corral was set up down below the tent area, to be replaced in a few days with a real wooden corral made from aspen and spruce logs. The experienced hands started laying out the kitchen tent and canvas fly. This was a key aim, given the rainy weather. Since I was a newbie at that point, I did what I was told. Take this, stretch this, carry this, etc.

I would suspect that several of the working wranglers took off down the trail to bring up more supplies, as that was a constant activity in those early days. I recall working on setting up some of the teepee tents, first making sure the ground was clear of obstructions, and as level as can be, also recall helping set up the 5'x7' (or was it 5'x8') wall tents. These wall tents were used for the paid hunters who were scheduled to show up in about 10 days. The hunter's tents were also canvas wall tents but were different in that they had a tent flap hole so that a small metal, wood stove could be installed for their comfort. One of my later jobs was to light some of those stoves each night, after supper, so the hunters were warm when they got undressed and slipped into their Eddie Bauer goose down sleeping bags. The paid hunter sleeping tents also had a wood frame in the floor (made with aspen trees) for each person sleeping in the tent. Inside the frame, we placed spruce boughs (leafy limbs) to make the beds more comfortable. I recall someone telling me to make sure the limbs were cut flat, not sharp ends, as that tends to puncture an air mattress. It was better for the limbs to be blunt ended.

Another job I specifically recall was assisting in building the more permanent corral. Luckily, we had tools like shovels, and a posthole digger that must have been among the equipment packed in, as I know there was a chainsaw, too. It just took a day or so to build the corral, as there were quite a few people working on it, with some cutting the poles, others (including me) digging the holes, etc. In no time, the corral was finished, and along with it, they set some logs up where the saddles could be placed when not being used, and to store other tack. Besides the large Kitchen tent, there were some other special purpose tents. One was used to store horse feed and related items, and another was located just above the kitchen area, was called the "gun tent". This was so the expensive firearms that the hunters were bringing, most of which included expensive optic scopes, could be stored, protected from rain and snow, but also at temperatures similar to hunting conditions, to help prevent them "fogging up" as can happen if they constantly go from very warm, to freezing temperature fluctuations.

While on this topic, it is important for me to talk about R.W.

Thomson's "gun rules". He was a very demanding person in some ways, and he had rules that not only his staff had to follow, but his paid hunters as well. Certainly, those of us who were family members were not exempt, perhaps held to a stricter standard than others, as I recall receiving several "stern lectures", mostly deserved. He did not just spring this on his hunters when they arrived at camp, but published them, before the hunters signed a reservation and deposit to attend one of his camps. On gun safety, he was adamant. Here are the key gun rules I recall:

1. A gun is ALWAYS loaded and must be treated as such. I recall as a child, when he was our next-door neighbor, he would read us the riot act if we even pointed a cap gun or BB gun at someone.

2. When a hunter comes into camp from hunting, and approaches the gun tent, he\she must unload all cartridges from the magazine, and chamber, and then point the gun to the sky, and dry fire the gun, to prove it was empty, before storing it in the gun tent.

3. Thomson had minimum caliber regulations, as he was a big proponent of using a weapon that had enough stopping power for the game targeted. His good friend Elmer Keith's similar viewpoint provides evidence of this, and they jointly developed the 338-378 KT towards that end. For example, if hunting elk, a 7mm or 300H&H, 338 or similar were allowed, but a 30-30, 30-06, and 270, were not. They could be used if just deer hunting, but not for elk. Legendary 270 proponent Jack O'Connor would not be allowed in Thomson's elk camp.

4. No alcohol allowed when out hunting, or when handling firearms. After the gun was put away, the brandy or rum or scotch was ok, but not before.

I remember rule #2 being talked about by others, and confirmation that multiple times through the years, a hunter would do the dry fire procedure before placing the gun in the rack of the gun tent, and a loud BANG would happen. It did not happen during this 1972 camp that I recall, but apparently had in years past.

One job which was assigned specifically to my brother Dale, and myself was the construction of "toilet gulch". One of the older teepee tents was designated as the "toilet" tent, in the Ft. Defiance 1972 camp. It was located about 50 yards south of the big kitchen tent, in a small side gulch. This toilet teepee tent was a modified version from the ones we used for sleeping, in that its bottom was cut with flaps so that its floor could accommodate the placement of a toilet, but still provide for a floor. My brother was assigned the task of building of a frame for the toilet seat, which was to be affixed to the frame. My primary task, thankfully, was digging the hole that was deep enough to contain the expected output from 20 to 30 inhabitants of our encampment. Luckily, I had a shovel and a posthole digger, and even though the work was hard, I know I was thankful for not being involved in construction of the toilet box, as I have no ability in construction then, or even now, fifty years later, none of those skills have I mastered. After the hole was dug, and the tent was placed over the spot, we placed the completed toilet box, over the hole, added a post nearby that had a nail on its end, to hold a roll of TP, and added a nearby box of lime with a small cup, so each user could sprinkle a little lime, to keep the smell reasonable, and we considered the job complete.

To our misfortune, the first to use our feat of engineering was none other than our Uncle Bob. When he was done, we were summoned by Bob, where we received one of his legendary lectures of our complete failure of toilet engineering, filled with a variety of cusswords that only a veteran of the US Navy could have mastered, the toilet construction allowed one to sit down, and perform #2 activities in an OK manner, but not so well to allow the pee to flow downward in a complete, unobstructed manner, i.e. because of how close the seat was positioned too close to the front of the box, Thomson had peed all over himself. Re-Engineering of the seat location to allow more room for the male genitals was required, and we both were happy when that task was completed. One did not enjoy receiving those lectures. In later years, my brother would become quite skilled in carpentry, and even worked for a time in that endeavor.

The primary focus within the camp's daily life was centered on the big kitchen tent, as previously mentioned it was at least 16'x20' in size, and was originally a US Army surplus type tent, with the typical green Army color. Outside the entrance of the tent was a large canvas "fly" that enabled an adjacent area to the kitchen where both hunters and staff could sit around an evening fire, with stumps to sit on, etc. Also, on the right side of the Kitchen tent exterior, was a table area with some washbasins, where a person could wash up. There was usually a large pot of hot water that one could pour into a washbasin, mix with spring water, and clean up. I guess one could shave there, but during my 1.5 months there, I recall little shaving, taking place. We used the same wash area in the evenings as the dishwashing area to clean up, and my recollection was that dishwashing chore was alternated among most of the crew, even some of the paid hunters.

As one entered the Kitchen tent, to the immediate left was the woodpile, at least that part of the wood supply protected from the elements. To the immediate right of the door and extending at least two-thirds the length of the tent, was a large table where many of the hunters and staff would eat meals. On the left side, towards the middle was the large cookstove, which was a 55-gal steel drum, with a welded flat cooking area on top, with stovepipe in the back, which extended up through a hole in the tent, for that purpose. I believe there was a way to bake as well, perhaps a Dutch oven, just can't recall that detail. Past the stove on the left and encompassing the back area of the tent; was where most of the stores and food supplies were kept. Besides all the staples, there were many boxes of snacks, such as raisins, candy bars, apples, etc. I particularly remember many packages of Baby Ruth's, Snickers, etc.

Breakfast was typically eggs and bacon, biscuits, although sometimes we could have oatmeal, cereal, or flapjacks too. Lunches were much less formal, sandwiches, candy bar and/or apple, as when people were out scouting or hunting, they would take a sandwich or two that the cooks had prepared, plus the snacks and apple.

Suppers were more sit down, and included a variety of items, like roast beef and potatoes, or steak, with several sides and desserts. I once recall, a full turkey dinner, with the fixings. Typically, after supper was when the stories would be told, the ones about the bull or buck that got away, and Matt and Jim would spin their tales as well.

During the time I was at camp, we had several different cooks and cook's helpers involved in kitchen operations. One person I remember was Don Hogan, who had been a cordon bleu chef in various places around the country, including some really nice hotel dining rooms and worked at the Red Steer in that capacity for several years. I don't think he was up at camp the whole time, just part time, my recollection being that he would work the busy weekends at the Red Steer, and come to camp, for several days at a time, when he could. Another cook from the Red Steer, Gary Amadeo, I recall being there also, but just at the beginning setup stage. Several other cooks, both sisters, Sue, and Lynn Bolinger, worked a major portion of the camp primarily as cooks. In later years, I would get to know both Don and Gary very well and went fishing with both many times on the Roaring Fork and Colorado Rivers.

Once the camp was primarily set up, the daily work routine for me and my brother comprised these general activities:

Get woke up before daybreak, usually by seventy-three-year-old Matt Buttram, and he would say something like: "Wake up boys, your burning daylight", "we got to take care of these horses", or "time to feed the ponies."

- Have breakfast. Sometimes this was before horses came in, other times later, depending how far the horses had wandered during the night.

- Once the cowboys had located the horses (most had been hobbled with leather front foot cuffs that restricted their movement, some of them had "bells" on, so the wranglers could find them easier, often they could be a half mile or further away. The process of finding them, and bringing them back, was called "jingling". So, we would wait by the corral, and we would open the corral, as the cowboys drove them in, then close the corral up when they were all in.

- Next, we (and other staff) would put lead ropes on their halters, and go through putting the saddle blankets on, saddle them, bridles, etc.

- The rest of morning we would do tasks as directed. Usually this was stuff like filling water containers at the spring, carrying it to the kitchen tent, filling the containers, etc.

- Often, we would help with moving wood from the main woodpile that Jim Buttram (Age 86) would cut and split daily, and move it to the kitchen wood pile.

- When Jim's woodpile would diminish, we would help with bringing dead wood from the surrounding hillsides. Usually, one of us would go with Matt Buttram, who would be on horseback, and we would go 100-200 yards up in the mostly aspen covered hills surrounding camp. A suitable dead aspen tree would be found, then Matt would throw out a loop from his rope, and we would put the loop around the butt end of the log. Matt would then loop his end of the rope around his saddle horn and drag it down to where Jim's woodpile was (about 20 feet to the right of the spring), whereupon the other brother would remove the loop, return it to Matt, and move the log to the pile, and we would repeat the cycle, until we had enough wood. I never really thought about it then, but we were two sets of brothers, about 50 years in age difference, working together in that camp.

- Generally, help with getting horses saddled/unsaddled, hobbling them (and un-hobbling), sometimes giving the "night horses" some Omolene feed. Night horses are the ones kept in the corral overnight, so the cowboys could ride them early in the morning to catch the ones that were out there (hobbled, some with bells) and feeding.

- In the evening, right after supper, we would often gather up small pieces of cut firewood, and go to the paid hunter's tents, and light their small tent stoves, to make sure their tents were nice and toasty. Our teepee tents did not have stoves, but after 5 minutes the goose down bags kept us warm.

Below is a picture of Matt and Jim Buttram, taken about three months after the 1972 Defiance camp. As mentioned before, Jim was age 86 in that Defiance camp, and baby brother Matt was a mere 73 years old. Both worked very hard, but I believe that they were hired as much for their entertainment and storytelling abilities as the hard work they provided. Anyway, Jim was an old muleskinner, an experienced coal miner, and for a brief time, had taken care of sheep. So, to Matt, who was an old traditional cowboy, and looked like an "older" version of the Marlboro man, who thought his older brother Jim was nothing but a "goldarn'd sheepherder", low on the totem pole as could be. And Matt would remind Jim about being a "sheepherder" almost daily. Anyway, they kept things lively around the supper meal in the evenings.

Matt Buttram (left), Jim Buttram (right). Photo taken by family, in 1973, Daniel Parliman, digital image.

One story that Jim would tell was the reason he left Arkansas and came to Colorado as a young man. The reason, he said, was because he raised too much hell in Arkansas, one of the final reasons is that he rode into church because he was mad at the preacher, and fired his guns in the church, and so they had warrants out against him.

I don't want to imply that all we did was work. We had a decent amount of time during the day to scout the country, either on foot or horseback, especially after the initial work of camp setup was complete. We also sometimes would help ferry supplies up and down the trail. One day, I was assigned in helping the more experienced cowboys with improving the trail, using shovels, and widening the trail in several places. Also, using bush cutters to reduce the thick buckbrush, before the hunters were to arrive. For that, we walked down the trail quite a way, then cut the brush back as we walked up. We did a bit of maintenance on some of the hunting trails as well. This would be a good time to show one of the hunter's maps that Thomson would provide for them. This is one of the Ft. Defiance maps:

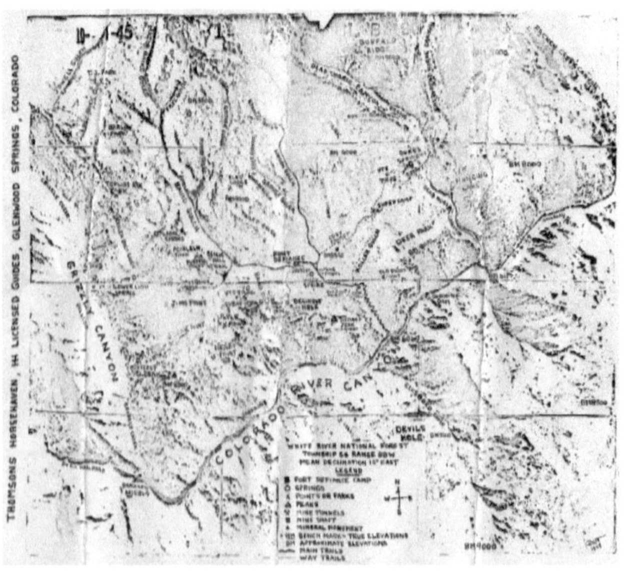

Ft. Defiance Hunting Area Map drawn by Robert W. Thomson; Daniel Parliman digital image.

Where the map shows "Ft. Defiance", was where camp was located. At the bottom of the map is the Colorado River canyon, called Glenwood Canyon. That was the sixty-six-switchback trail, previously described, which we originally used to bring all the people and equipment into camp. To our north (right on the map) was a substantial canyon called "Deadhorse Canyon". It was mostly impassible for us to access, but there was one trail that crossed it, but I never traveled that far. Deadhorse is also where the present-day tourist attraction of Hanging Lake is located. A very picturesque day hike. There is a present day exit on I-70 that provides access, although I have heard that you must now get tickets in advance if you wish to do that hike.

To the left on the map was an even more deep canyon, called Grizzly Creek Canyon. The area to the northwest went a very long way before one would hit a paved road, although there was a dirt road that was open in summer that went towards Deep Lake and beyond. Looking at current maps, it is roughly at least 15+ square miles of hunting area even if you take out the steep canyon areas of the Colorado, Deadhorse and Grizzly Creek canyons.

The following is who I believe were the staff who worked that camp. I sure hope I am not forgetting any of the great people at that camp, but based on my memory, and asking a few others that were there, here is my best recollection of staff; besides my uncle Robert W. Thomson, and my aunt, Jean Thomson, and my brother Dale, and myself (note: not all staff stayed the entire time):

Wranglers\Guides: Jim Brink, Ron Brink, Zella Brink, Charlie Bolinger, Don VanLandingham, Chuck "Choddy" Petersen, Tom Mitchell

Kitchen (Chefs, Cooks, Kitchen helpers): Don Hogan, Gary Amadeo, Lynn Bolinger, Sue Bolinger, K.? Mitchell

#1 Woodcutter and storyteller: Jim Buttram

Senior Cowboy in charge of wood gathering and wake-up calls of

Jersey Dudes: Matt Buttram

I do not recall the names of the various paid hunters in that camp, although I recall several were from the Chicago area, and I know that one of them was Ted Keith, from Idaho, who bagged a very nice mule deer buck. Ted was the son of Thomson's good friend, Elmer Keith (Gun editor of Guns & Ammo Magazine.) Elmer and his wife, Lorraine, did also attend the later part of the hunt (and had hunted with Thomson several previous years). My recollection is that we had about 15-20 paid hunters that year.

My recollection is we filled all the elk tags of the paid hunters (some were cow elk, as some hunters had drawn cow elk permits that year too), and I recall quite a few bucks were brought down the mountain that fall as well.

I would like to finish up this article by relating a few specific stories that I recall from that 1972 hunting camp.

Packing Dan's Buck to Camp

This is not a hunting story per se, although it was my actual very first bagging of a deer (preceded as described earlier about the Buffalo and Antelope a few months before). I had hunted a good bit as a young man, both for small game and large, and did hunt for about 10 years after this trip, and still enjoy fly fishing.

While we were up in Defiance, we sometimes hunted together in small groups, or sometimes my brother and I would hunt together, and sometimes by ourselves. On this day, I was hunting alone, on horseback, and headed east, along the Ute Trail, past what we called "Cozy Pocket". I then I veered off the trail somewhat south, in the general direction of Deadhorse Canyon, to an area of semi-open, mixed aspen and buckbrush, named by my uncle as "Deer Park". It was a mile, maybe a little less, from camp. Fifty years later, I cannot remember which rifle I had, although I think it was the old 30-40 Kraig lever action, but could have been my uncle's 300 H&H. Anyway, after I had dismounted and was walking around, I spooked a small 4-point buck, although body wise was a decent sized buck, who started to run slowly, and I was fortunate to shoot him, I think maybe it was the second shot. Where he ended up was on a little island within the buckbrush that had a few trees, mostly spruce trees. I quickly field dressed him and leaned him on a dead tree in a nice shady area, and went back to camp. The weather was cool then and did not have any fears about the meat spoiling but was taught that leaving any meat out too long could sometimes attract bears.

It was the next morning, or the day after that, we planned to go back and collect my buck and add him back to the camp's growing meat pole. By this time, I was getting more experience at packing, but still had packed no game out by myself. Two of the cowboys (I wish I could recall their names!) were assigned to ride with me, and I was provided with one of our two small pack mules as my pack animal. Mule Deer were typically cut in half, and would fit nicely on one pack animal, each half in one pannier. One thing I should mention is that we had two of these small mules in camp, and those two were very attached to one another, what one would call "inseparable". Their names were: "Don" and "Marcia". As the three of us rode out of camp, the mule did a fair amount of "braying", but he came along, and after a few hundred yards seemed to settle down. Not sure if I had "Don", or "Marcia", but that pair did not like to be separated.

I was in the lead, with the mule's lead rope in my right hand, followed by the two wranglers. Just as I had done before, went east along the Ute trail, and at the appropriate place diverted more south towards Deer Park. After a while, as we approached the area where my buck was aging on the tree shaded island, I spied movement in front of me, to my left. To my surprise, I saw a big buck running towards Deadhorse Canyon, not just any buck, but a huge one with an ultra-wide rack, bigger than any I have ever seen (before or since), even in any outdoor magazines, etc. I dropped my lead rope to the mule, pulled my rifle from the scabbard, got off my horse, and tried to get a shot off, but he was gone!

And not only was the big buck gone, but the damned mule took off running the other way! Now normally if you drop a lead rope, the animal will invariably step on it, and is relatively easy to catch. But that s-o-b was running back towards camp, like it was Secretariat (which won the triple crown less than a year later). The two wranglers were laughing their asses off, and probably making references about the "Jersey Dude" which was a common thing my brother and I had to endure, that fall. They said something to the effect that they would wait there, so I could go retrieve the wayward mule.

I had to go all the way back to camp, where the damned mule was standing next to his buddy mule. Hard to remember now, but the two wranglers were probably still laughing when I finally got back to "deer park". Anyway, we packed the deer out with no further incident, except my hurt pride. I returned to Defiance in the following several years, archery hunting, and while successful, never saw THAT big old buck again.

Heart Attack

While the paid hunters were in camp, one thing that happened that caused some temporary excitement was that one hunter became ill and complained of chest pains. My recollection was the hunter was from the Chicago area. The camp doctor felt that the situation called for medical attention, so it was decided to carry him down the sixty-six switchbacks to seek medical attention. Someone fashioned a litter made from Aspen trees cut for that purpose, and six of the camp cowboys volunteered to carry him down the mountain, which they did, and got him to Valley View Hospital in Glenwood Springs. Luckily, my understanding was that it was not serious, perhaps indigestion, but better to be safe in a situation like that.

After the camp was over, the hunter who was carried down the mountain trail sent each of the stretcher bearers a portable color TV.

Nunny's Cave Spring

Ever since I first heard stories about Ft. Defiance back home in New Jersey at the Colorado Café, I had heard about a magical place named "Nunny's Cave Spring." It was described as a rock cave, almost big enough to walk into standing up, that contained a stream of crystal clear, cold water gushing out of the rock, forming a small stream, and then cascading down the canyon.

Nunny was my mother's brother nickname, real name (rarely used) was Henry DeCinque Jr. He was a very experienced hunter, preferring to go hunting afoot, exploring, and finding unknown places. He had hunted in the Defiance country several years during the later 1950s, in Thomson's camp, and after 1960 in Avalanche Canyon areas when Thomson shifted operations there. A bit later in the 60s, Nunny then started doing his own camps with his good friend Sam Azeez, also of South Jersey, and because of that, became estranged from Bob Thomson for a few years. As far as I am aware, Nunny never returned to Defiance after the early 1960s, but as a child, I had heard the stories about his "cave spring".

The basic story (this took place in the late 1950s) was that Nunny was out exploring one day along the canyon rim, and saw down below him, several mule deer, milling about. He climbed down the canyon, and as he climbed down, through a very steep slope, discovered this cave, as described, with gushing cold water, etc.

The story continued as he went back to Defiance camp, told his father Henry Sr. and his uncle Bob Thomson about it, who could not believe the story. Both had hunted the Defiance area for 10+ years at that point, and never had they or anyone else reported it. So next day, Nunny took his father and uncle to the area, and tried to take a path to the cave that was easier for his older relatives to follow, he led them down via an easier and less steep path, until they both were to confirm that yes indeed, there was a "Nunny's Cave Spring."

Before they left, Henry Sr. took out one of his (then) company business cards, and wrote on the back of it, something to the effect that "whoever finds this card, can send it to me, and I will pay you $100.00" and he put the card inside the cave on a shelf, and weighed down the card, with a rifle cartridge.

No one ever sent him that card.

DECINQUE OIL COMPANY
DISTRIBUTORS
PETROLEUM PRODUCTS

HENRY DECINQUE

CAPE MAY COURT HOUSE, N. J.
CAPE MAY COURT HOUSE 5-3931

Example of H. DeCinque business card, similar to the one left in the cave. Daniel Parliman Digital image.

During the 1972 camp, on one of the days I was in that area with some others, we went down looking for that cave spring, and after a lot of climbing, and searching, we did indeed find it, and it was just as described. Also, the amount of climbing, steep climbing was just as described. Especially climbing back out. The amount of water was impressive, I actually thought at the time, that if someone could ever put some cutthroat trout in that little stream, they might just be able to survive, as I saw water insects and "flies" hatching just like on trout streams I was familiar with.

Naturally, I searched for Grandpa's business card and cartridge but could not find it. The one real regret I have, is that I did not take a picture of the Nunny's Spring Cave, perhaps someday, someone will do so and send it to me, but it is nice for there to still exist some secret places, to which only a few have so far traveled. I wondered if the Ute Native Americans ever had tasted the sweet water of this spring? They certainly could have, but there were enough other springs in the general area that the trip to the cave would have been a chore, even for them, compared to other water sources. I have searched on the internet, but have never seen a picture posted, so far, of that cave.

Nunny found another secret cave in a different part of the Flattops, in a different year (probably also before 1960), this one had Native American painting on the walls, and although I know approximately about where it was supposed to be located, I have never yet visited that one. We will keep that one secret, too.

Packing Up, Final thoughts

There were several groups of hunters that year in camp, including a "late hunt", and my memory of the success overall was that all the paid hunter elk tags were filled, several of which were of cow elk, which was prized by many for its flavor.

I only harvested that one buck that year, as previously mentioned, but my brother was successful in getting two mule deer bucks and a nice spike bull elk. In later years I was to come back to Ft. Defiance both on backpacking trips and fall archery hunts, and although we were successful several times, never saw that gigantic buck I had previously seen that caused me to lose the pack mule!

Elmer Keith hunted with my uncle during the latter part of the season. I do not recall details about his hunt, but recall that Elmer's son Ted harvested a real nice mule deer buck in the earlier part of the season.

My Uncle, R.W. (Bob) Thomson did in fact bag a nice bull elk while hunting the "Big Buck Ridge" area at long range (approx. 600 yards) using his .338-.378 rifle during that 1972 Last Thomson Camp. He had it mounted and overlooked the salad bar in the Red Steer Restaurant until fire unfortunately destroyed the restaurant in 1979.

One of the major benefits to me of the entire Last Thomson Hunting Camp was all the great experiences encountered up there, besides the specific stories I have mentioned. Here are a few remembrances:

- Enjoyed learning to not only how to ride a horse, but how to pack a horse\mule, including how to tie a double-diamond hitch, which in later years would be useful in several trips of my own on the Flattops.

- The cowboys and camp staff treated us very well, although we were fair game for a variety of New Jersey and Eastern Dude references, talk about "snipe hunts" which we did not believe, also were reminded to say "WAHTER" not "WOODER" as we grew up speaking about "water". Also, if we were drinking a soft drink, it was POP, not SODA.

- Seeing various wildlife, like porcupines, grouse, hawks, besides the elk and deer big game animals. I recall vividly watching a hawk attempt to catch a snowshoe hare that was running across an opening, and when he failed to nail him in the oak brush, the hawk tried chasing him on foot, but was not rewarded with a meal in that instance.

- The (mostly) beautiful blue-sky weather of the fall, with golden aspen trees intermixed with green spruce trees, and the occasional snowfall to add contrast to the scene.

- I had heard the stories growing up in NJ about the not so bright grouse they had in Colorado. How a person, could shoot a bunch of them, if you wanted to, simply start at the bottom of tree, and work up, just so the remaining birds don't see them dropping in front of them, as opposed to the ruffled grouse in South Jersey, who flush away, when you get to within 70 yards.

After the camp was over, the equipment taken down, and hauled away, and the meat processed, you would have thought we would have rested the next several months. Instead, Uncle Bob, bought us shotguns, we hunted ducks multiple times, pheasants down near Rifle, CO, attempted to go goose hunting near Ft. Collins, and attended the National Western Stock Show in Denver. We also were working at the restaurant every night, except Mondays, and during 1973 New Year's weekend, Uncle Bob booked the forties vocal group, "The Ink Spots" so they could usher in the New Year at the Red Steer, to a full house. My "job" for that event was operating the spotlight as they sang "When the Saints Come Marching In" and other tunes. It was a hectic six months for some Jersey Dudes.

Read On to the AFTERWARD…

Robert W. Thomson, family photo, c. 1966, Daniel Parliman, digital image. This photo taken in the Avalanche Creek Hunting area.

AFTERWARD

The Thomson hunting camp of fall 1972 was "The Last Thomson Hunting Camp" because **Robert W. Thomson,** passed away a few months later, in late January 1973, at age 52. He had scarlet fever as a young child which the doctor told him he would not live a long life and was told he could not take part in sports (he played high school and college basketball, supposedly asking a friend to take his sports physical to get around that issue) but that condition, combined with 4+ packs of Camel cigarettes a day and too much scotch, no doubt shortened his life. After his Memorial service, he was cremated, and later that year, his ashes were placed in a Colorado wilderness location by close friends and family during the summer of 1973, including his brother-in-law, Henry DeCinque, Sr. and other family members, including this author. His wife Jean carried on the restaurant business in Glenwood Springs for many years, joined by several of Jean's sisters, Helen and Gloria, along with Gloria's spouse, Carl Sehl, until their retirement. All the sisters have unfortunately now passed away, the last, in 2019.

On June 17, 1977, Jim Buttram's baby brother **Mathew Buttram** was killed outside a bar in Glenwood Springs, Colorado. He was 77 years old.

Bob's brother, **R. James "Jim" Thomson**, of Evergreen, Colorado, passed away on December 25, 2003. As a young man, he was an integral part of the Thomson trail rides and worked as a surveyor in his early years. He attended Mesa College and graduated from the University of Colorado with honors. He married his Glenwood Springs sweetheart, H. Marie Gamba in 1940. She preceded him in death in 1974. Mr. Thomson worked for many years as the chief engineer with Stearns-Rogers Mining and Manufacturing Corp., contributing many innovations and inventions during his tenure, and is survived by sons, daughters, and grandchildren.

Around 1979, **Henry DeCinque Sr.** then in his 70s, took part in his last Colorado hunt, and his first, since his last Thomson hunting camp, joining brother-in-law Carl Sehl, and grandson Daniel Parliman in a horseback camp in the Colorado Flattops. Daniel positioned his grandfather in one likely spot near a beautiful aspen park, overlooking a timbered gulch, and his uncle Carl at another position higher up the ridge, then circled around into a stand of dark timber where a small herd of elk spooked and ran in several ways, primarily towards Henry. Soon, several shots rang out from his Winchester .338 model 70 rifle. Henry had bagged a nice bull elk, but had dropped his pipe on the ground, and was cussing his disappointment to Daniel when he rode up, because he could only get one of the two bulls that had run out of the timber towards him, as he was trying to light his pipe.

James "Jim" Buttram passed away at age 96, in 1982. His obituary mentioned his work in coal mines, his love for hunting and horses, and his professional horseshoeing. It did not mention the brief time herding sheep. The "hog-law" strategy had worked out.

Elmer Keith, friend of R.W. Thomson, co-creator of the 338-378 KT cartridge, and dean of the Gun Writers of the twentieth century (many give him credit as the driving force for the release of the .44 magnum), passed away in February 1984. He was author of about 10 books related to hunting and Guns (see Bibliography)

George G. Shaw, friend of both Rich and Robert W. Thomson, long time rodeo clown, hunting guide, horseman, and entertainer, passed in July 1993. He was also a WWII vet (Navy), and Korea vet (Marines).

Thurman "Fum" McGraw, friend of Robert W. Thomson, and supplier of horses and tack to the Thomson Hunting Camps, and legendary College Hall of Fame football player, passed on in September 2000. His beloved wife Brownie, passed away in March 2020. I happened to sit next to Fum when he attended the memorial for R.W. Thomson at the Red Steer Restaurant, in January 1973. What a great, interesting person he was!

July 30, 2002 - **Henry DeCinque Sr**. passed away peacefully one day before his 93rd birthday, after a long career as an independent oil distributer in Cape May County NJ, well-known pioneer aviator, and participant in about 30 hunting trips to Colorado. After his funeral service, he was also cremated. After several years, several of his grandsons, both Parliman and DeCinque, and other family and friends, got together a wilderness pack trip, placed his ashes in their final resting place, right next to brother-in-law and good friend, R.W. Thomson; both sets of ashes forever located together in the Colorado Rocky Mountain wilderness, they both so deeply loved. His spouse, **Estelle**, passed away in 2009, at age 97. They are survived by a daughter, 9 grandchildren, and great grandchildren.

Henry DeCinque Jr. (Nunny) passed away in June 2014 at age 75, survived by his spouse, sons, daughters, and grandchildren.

Unfortunately, the **Grizzly Creek Fire of 2020,** which took several months to fully contain, looks to have damaged a wide area of what I would define as the Ft. Defiance hunting camp area. The fire damaged over 32,000 acres (50 square miles)! I have checked it out on Google Earth, the damage is very extensive. I know the area will recover, as the winter snowpack, the buckbrush, aspen trees, and the Engelman spruce trees will rehabilitate the land. Hopefully that ultra-wide buck's genetic material still lives on in its descendants.

To let us know your comments on this book, please provide a review at either Amazon.com or Goodreads.com. Feedback is appreciated!

To contact the author directly, we would enjoy your comments, and pictures; and plan to post additional information related to this book: https://grizzlycreekpublishing.com/

Also, you are invited to please join our Facebook group: https://www.facebook.com/groups/storiesoftheamericanwest

DANIEL PARLIMAN, FLOWERY BRANCH, GEORGIA, JANUARY 14, 2023

BIBLIOGRAPHY

Much information about **Rich Thomson's early life** can be found in older newspapers, searching for "Rich Thomson" or Rich Roy Thomson", particularly in newspaper archives of western Colorado, and especially newspapers in Glenwood Springs, Grand Junction, and Aspen. One such resource:

https://www.coloradohistoricnewspapers.org/

A search for "Rich Thomson" with no date, will find over 200 results. To find mostly rodeo, cowboy type of results, restrict results to before 1907, which is when he joined the Forest Service. An interesting one is to look at the 1904 articles, and these stand out:

Rocky Mountain News Aug. 28, 1904, and also Avalanche Echo Sept 1, 1904 – which describes Rich's exploits at winning the saddle bronc title and other contests

Additional Information for **Robert W. Thomson (RWT):**

Article in "Guns & Ammo" by RWT February 1967 "Hit them at 300 yards+" Describes his **"Colorado Double Dot Long Range"** system.

Guns & Ammo Article May 1968 by Gun Editor Elmer Keith, on **"Birth of a 500 Yard Elk Buster"** details the background of the development 338-378 KT cartridge (Keith-Thomson), detailing the background of the development of that cartridge by Elmer Keith, and Robert W. Thomson

1974 Guns & Ammo Annual, p154-158 **"Our last Rifle"** Describes by Elmer Keith the joint contribution of he, Bob Thomson, and Jerry Haskins in developing a custom rifle designed to use the 338-378KT cartridge. Article written and published after R.W. Thomson's passing.

Elmer Keith, in addition to his numerous magazine articles where he discussed **R.W. Thomson** and their common love for using large caliber magnum cartridges, also mention Thomson (sometimes misspelled as Thompson) in several of his books, including:

"Keith, an Autobiography." Winchester Press, 1974, pp.359-361, 366, 373

"Hell, I was there!" Illustrated large Print. Petersen Publishing Company, 1979 Many references to R.W. Thomson throughout Chapter 8 pp.269-308 including very detailed photos of Elmer and/or Lorraine with Bob, many of them at Thomson's Avalanche or Ft. Defiance Hunting Camps. Photos on pages: 271, 284, 288, 299, 306. In the 1972 Last Thomson Hunting Camp, both Elmer's son Ted, and Elmer, were among Thomson's hunters.

The book: "American Mountain People" by "National Geographic Society" Photographer: **Bruce Dale** Copyright 1973 pp150-151 Caption reads: "Pack train of elk hunters edge up a chaparral-covered hillside as a freight train passes through Colorado's Glenwood Canyon

Note about the photo: Most of the other riders in that photo are obscured, although if you look real careful, you will see a rider behind Jean and Bob, maybe 20+ feet with a dark hat and blaze orange slicker, right in the buckbrush) well that was 16 year old me, with I believe my 15 year old brother Dale, in the brush ahead of me. To the very far right is one of the wranglers, I cannot absolutely identify, but wearing a bright yellow slicker, it might be Zella Brink - it rained quite a lot that trip up the 66 switchbacks of the trail, from the bottom of Glenwood Canyon, up to the Defiance hunting camp. In later years, I also backpacked up that trail several times in the 70s, I think in the several hours spent walking up each time, there would typically be at least 3-6 trains going thru the Canyon, during the hike. Especially since the Grizzly Fire of 2020 I would expect there is no real trail left, do not try unless you check with Forest Service first.

Info on the White River National Forest:

https://www.fs.usda.gov/whiteriver

Info on the Flattops Wilderness Area:

https://www.fs.usda.gov/recarea/whiteriver/recarea/?recid=81112

Wikipedia Information on the Grizzly Creek Fire of 2020:

https://en.wikipedia.org/wiki/Grizzly_Creek_Fire

For more about the history of the Trail Riders of the wilderness, check out this link on the web:

https://foresthistory.org/digital-collections/pioneer-trail-riders-of-the-wilderness/

Glenwood Springs Photographer **John B. Schutte**, took many hundreds (thousands?) of photos during the Thomson Trail Rides, and as far as I could research, those photos can be found in several collections, but very few of them are available online. Perhaps someday that will change. For more information, please check with the following organizations, each of which may have some of those photos:

Denver Public Library:
https://archives.denverlibrary.org/repositories/3/resources/7022

Frontier Historical Society, Glenwood Springs, CO
https://www.glenwoodhistory.com/

Aspen Historical Society, Aspen, CO
https://aspenhistory.org/

For those looking to participate in a trail ride within the Flattops or nearby areas, I might suggest that AJ Brink Outfitters be considered for one of their customizable Trail Ride Trips.

Web Link: https://brinkoutfitters.com/

Please say hello, and check for any updated information, and more (mostly color) related photos, also planning to add a few video clips of the Ft. Defiance hunting camp films I have digitized :

https://grizzlycreekpublishing.com/

You are also invited to please join our Facebook group: https://www.facebook.com/groups/storiesoftheamerican west

Several of the wranglers at Avalanche Camp, DeCinque Meadow. c. 1967. Family photo Daniel Parliman Digital Photo

9 798218 124182